Psalm 127:1

·Except the Lord build the house, they labour in vain that build it: except the Lord keep the city, the watchman waketh but in vain..

Southern Crossing

"Ithaca's Legacy"

by

Randall Franks

One of America's favorite TV cops and country

music entertainers shares a Southern police drama.

Peach Picked Publishing
ISBN: 979-8-9926585-0-7
P.O. Box 42, Tunnel Hill, Georgia 30755

Photos, drawings or any artworks unless otherwise noted
© Randall Franks Media

Front cover headshot: Randall Franks Media/Anna Ritch

Dedicated to

my friend
fellow actor/screenwriter
Alan Autry

and
In Remembrance

of
**Carroll O'Connor,
Peter Salim, Jill Freeman**

and
my father
Floyd Franks
who bought my
first
1940 Royal Typewriter

Southern Crossing

Forward

My adventures in participating in stage productions go back to my early elementary school years. Within our imaginations we created our own adventures and played them out to make the days pass with greater interest.

After God opened the doors to me of the magical world of film and television and allowed me to become part of the brotherhood of the Lion, it is amazing what gifts of learning were imparted to me. When I say the brotherhood of the Lion, that is how I refer to my five years at the MGM University of Atlanta by becoming part of the long list of actors and crew who had gainful employment from the legendary film studio MGM/UA. This is a family tradition of sorts as I had several of my cousins who also shared this privilege beginning with silent film veteran Buster Keaton, to Golden Era stars Jimmy Stewart, Katharine Hepburn, Lucille Ball, and Shirley Temple.

I became one of the young knights of the stage used by TV icon Carroll O'Connor and the producers to entertain 25 million Americans and millions in 150 countries around the world on the drama "In the Heat of the Night."

I desired to expand my knowledge on many fronts, acting, directing, lighting, camera and even screenwriting. I will never forget after reading script after script, deciding I also had stories to share. So, in my free time, I took out the black cast iron 1940 Royal typewriter that my father got me years earlier and began tapping out the story within my head and heart.

"Ithaca's Legacy"

Using the TV script format as a model, I soon had the flow of what I wanted to share and the story fell easily off the ends of my fingers as the typewriter ribbon filled each page until I completed four acts for a one-hour TV episode.

With script in hand, I really didn't know what was next. So, I began to ask others who were more accustomed to reading hundreds of these to review my efforts. Initially, the director of photography Peter Salim accommodated me and gave me his criticisms, then the script supervisor Jill Freeman, who provided some candid advice on my approach. Then I shared it with my co-star Alan Autry, who added more encouragement until I finally got the nerve to give it to Carroll. That choice then allowed Carroll to provide me some of my greatest lessons in screenwriting.

While that script never made it to screen, it was my true beginning in screenwriting. I would go on to write several more for stage, movies, sitcoms, TV dramas, both on my own and in partnership with others.

Just like a songwriter, perfecting a song over time, a script never really is finished until it reaches the stage, film or tape. And even at the point of committal, it still is improved and rewritten to enhance the heart and soul of the project to move the audience.

This novella "Southern Crossing" is based upon a TV series concept that found its inspiration from that very first TV story that I typed upon the pages with my Royal. I hope within these pages you find characters of interest taking actions that will move your thoughts and your heart into a new locale which uplifts and inspires you to desire to not only read the words but to wish to walk alongside them.

Randall Franks

Major Charles Wilson

Chapter One

The moonless night sky hung heavy over Ithaca, casting dark shadows across the sprawling Southern estate.

Major Charles Wilson sat hunched over a counting desk in a cellar room, with the dim flicker of an oil lamp barely illuminating the ledger laid out before him. At thirty-five, Charles was tall and broad-shouldered, with a trim beard lining his angular jaw. His piercing blue eyes were fixed on the coins and the ledger laid out on the desk. He was the third-generation owner of Ithaca, having inherited the estate from his father, Daniel, Jr. For three generations, the Wilson family had built a life there since migrating from Jamestown, Virginia.

They constructed a magnificent manor house and village for the workers modeled after an Irish country estate described by their ancestor William, who had come to America from Ireland via the West Indies. He had been sent there enslaved as a political prisoner. He managed to work his way out of bondage and secured passage to Virginia.

Charles dipped his quill into an inkwell and carefully logged the latest figures below the date 7 May 1863, tallying the gold coins spread across the desk. As paymaster for the Western Confederate Army, it was Charles's solemn duty to safeguard the gold reserves. The scratching of the quill and the clinking of coins were punctuated by the muffled rat-a-tat-tat of artillery fire in the distance.

A creaking floorboard announced Willie's presence before the man emerged from the shadows. Charles didn't look up as Willie approached. He was shorter and stockier than the Major, with dark black skin and prominent cheekbones on his weathered face. His eyes shone with lively intellect.

"Major, the Yankees are just up the road!" Willie urged, a note of panic in his hushed voice.

Charles paused and glanced up at the daguerreotype of he, his wife and children sitting atop the desk. "Did you get our families off to Jackson?" he asked calmly, still facing away from Willie.

"Yes sir," came the reply from behind.

The barrage of gunfire was growing louder now; sporadic pops were blossoming into rolling volleys. Charles could delay no longer. He swept the remaining coins into a leather sack and hid them away with the others. He turned to his old friend.

"Willie, we have to get this ledger to General Pemberton at Vicksburg," he said briskly, tucking the book under his arm. "He has to know where I've stored the gold." Charles slipped three coins into his pocket before blowing out the lamp.

The two men stole into the muggy night air,

keeping to the shadows as they crept toward the stables behind the looming house. In the distance, the front gates framed a carved stone plaque reading "Ithaca 1820."

Charles cast a mournful glance back at the stately white columns and grand portico that had welcomed generations of Wilsons. There was no time for nostalgia now.

With crackling gunfire echoing ever nearer, Charles and Willie broke into a sprint, racing for the horses. It was too late – the intruders were already upon them.

"Halt!" barked a Yankee soldier as three blue-coated men burst from the shrubbery, rifles leveled. Charles ran headlong toward the stables, clutching his precious ledger like a life preserver. Willie's footfalls pounded behind him. Then, a deafening report split the night.

Searing pain exploded through Charles' chest as a musket ball found its mark. His breath escaped in a ragged gasp as he crumpled to the ground. Beside him, Willie collapsed mid-stride, felled by the vicious hail of lead.

The ledger slipped from Charles' limp fingers, falling open to reveal rows of numbers and scribbled notes. A few feet away, a gold coin winked in the moonlight, bearing the last traces of a doomed fortune. Above it all, the Yankees closed in through a thickening haze of gun smoke that choked the humid air. Charles' world faded into darkness, his mission a failure. But no one saw where he and Willie came from, and the ledger notes were coded so only he and the General might know their meaning. Charles had not yet passed the knowledge of the hiding place's existence to his heir, as his father had before him. Willie knew but also didn't share as he was sworn to secrecy. With their passing, while the mission was lost, its purpose was safeguarded from the enemy, so Charles and Willie did not give their lives in vain.

"Ithaca's Legacy"

Ithaca Gate

Chapter Two

The grand façade of Ithaca radiated the elegance and nobility of the Antebellum South, influenced by the descriptions handed down by William of the great house in Ireland he remembered from his youth. Six stately white columns lined the front portico, rising two stories to support a third-story widow's walk. The columns' smooth Doric design lent an air of restrained sophistication. Between the two center pillars, two imposing eight-foot doors with applied molding stood sentinel, their rich mahogany wood brought in by riverboat.

The mansion's brick walls were painted a pristine white and the many windows with their emerald shutters and decorative lintels reflected the symmetry favored by neoclassical architects. In the foreground near the entrance, a weathered stone archway welcomed guests through wrought iron gates. An engraved stone on the arch read "Ithaca 1820" in honor of the estate's founding.

Inside, a grand foyer with black and white marble floors greeted visitors. To the right, pocket doors opened to a stately parlor filled with baroque settees and curio cabinets polished to a high sheen. Across the foyer, the formal dining room dazzled with its Waterford crystal chandelier and hand-painted chinoiserie wallpaper.

A sweeping staircase with an ornately carved mahogany banister dominates the rear of the entry hall. Upstairs, family quarters evoked old-world charm with canopy beds, floral chaise lounges, and marble fireplaces carved from the finest Italian Carrara. The library's floor-to-ceiling built-in bookcases held leather-bound first editions and handwritten manuscripts preserved for posterity.

Throughout the home, fine art and portraits of progenitors past gazed down as a testament to the family's noble American lineage. Ithaca stood as a pinnacle of Southern splendor with a hint of old world influence. Despite the hard times of Reconstruction and the Great Depression, the Wilsons' unique model of operation had seen Ithaca thrive when others faded. Though they endured with less in the hard times like all their neighbors, expanding their product markets beyond the South, helped to keep Ithaca afloat. No slave had worked on the land since 1820, and then it was only those families who came from Virginia with Daniel, Sr. and Jr. in 1819. The laws of Virginia had not allowed Sr. to free the slaves he had inherited, but once he got to Mississippi and built his new home, he did.

All of those that came with him and wished it were given a life tenancy in a house in the new village built on the estate and hired for one of the many jobs needed to create the vision of Ithaca. The

Ithaca Village

family extended this tradition to each generation of their offspring, if they desired to stay and continue working. Alongside those that stayed, the family hired some Native Americans, some French, and Irish or Scots who wanted a new life in America, providing them housing as part of their employment.

Just beyond the manicured gardens of the grand manor lay the quaint Ithaca Village. The village was modeled after traditional Irish villages of the 1700s.

A winding dirt road led past simple whitewashed cottages with thatched roofs, chimneys of stone and wood, and brightly painted doors in cheery shades of blue and green.

The dirt floors more common in Ireland were replaced with solid foundations and floors of stone and wood. Ladder-back chairs lined up along the walls outside, where neighbors gathered to share the latest gossip. At the center of the village stood larger

Ithaca Village

workshop buildings built from local timber. The blacksmith's barn rang with the clanging of hammer on anvil as he shod horses and repaired tools. Inside the wood mill, saws cut timber. There was a grain-grinding mill by the creek, and workshops with every trade to create anything needed on the estate – a candle maker, a cobbler, a milliner, a potter, and a silver smith. The Wilsons lured master craftsmen to Ithaca and then paired young workers with them to continue in the trade as apprentices. Every generation passed their knowledge to the next.

Beyond the workshops sat a small stone chapel where villagers gathered every Sunday to give thanks. Everwood Hammond and then his son Clement and then his son Barton served as the village preacher, sharing the Word, marrying and burying through the years. The old faith had been left behind in Ireland; William's stand for his faith had cost him everything during the Second English Civil War. He did not intend for his offspring to ever again face that type of treatment by anyone, so when he reached America, he became a protestant.

During the week, they also worked the land. While they made everything they needed, they didn't stop there; their craftsmen worked constantly creating while the Wilson's sold everything with the Ithaca name attached.

Their products became sought after as the choice

of elegant buyers wherever the Wilson's could ship their wares. Under the model started by Daniel, everyone was paid, had a place to live, and shared in any profits of their contributing trade or specialty. It was the profit-sharing approach, which kept innovation and opportunity in the forefront of what they accomplished.

Like any Irish village, there was even a village tavern, and the Wilson's even created their own whiskey, beer, wines and sherries for use and sale from the estate.

This unique approach, gave Ithacans little need to deal with the happenings outside of their surroundings. Everyone lived together as neighbors, no matter their color, creed, or origin. If a malcontent found their way amongst them, they were soon dispatched on their way.

Surrounding the village were fertile fields where residents labored growing cotton, corn and other crops to support the estate. Simple homesteads dotted the pastures where farmhands tended to cattle and other livestock. There were fields for sheep worked by shepherds and dogs that housed seasonal sheering barns. They turned the wool into products to use and sell. There were fields for cattle with barns for milking. Their days began and ended with the chime of the village bell tower calling workers to the fields and shops. Between the village and the big house, stables housed the prized thoroughbred horses used to keep the farm going and the Wilson's riding in the finest style. Though the years provided a rustic and worn look, Ithaca Village provided community and a sense of belonging for multiple generations of workers loyal to the Wilson family legacy. Within its lasting charm reflected the Wilsons' roots across the sea. And that charm kept Ithaca an idyllic place even as it was catapulted into the civil unrest of the war of northern aggression; the unpleasantness of reconstruction and all the tumult that came to Mississippi for years to come.

Despite Charles's death in the Civil War, Ithaca remained an island, as his wife Ellen continued on eventually their oldest son Andrew would take over the estate. Upon his passing, Ithaca passed to the hands of his son Theodore. The Wilson's ran their estate like European Lords – father to eldest son – keeping the unpleasantness and cruelty of the world from all their doors. Each generation worked to create business opportunities at Ithaca or away from the estate for any other surviving children or their husbands. This approach worked well, as they held on through sending men to WWI – Martin O'Halahan and Tillman Fox did not return but monuments were raised to their memories beside the chapel. There were many lost dear ones during the Spanish Flu epidemic of 1918. There was Willa Branch and

three of her children Elly, Mary and Suzy. Nan
Robinson was the first to be hit but she fought it off,
an amazing deed at 70, and she was back to spin-
ning in no time. Sadly, the chapel cemetery saw several uplifted stones during that time. Even the Great
Depression was weathered better than the outside
world. Theodore Wilson had taken many of the
profits from their efforts and invested well in cotton
mills, foundries and other endeavors being blessed
to get out before the 1929 stock market fall. He also
was not a truster of banks, so he survived the bank
failures that came in the early 1930s. So, through
wise management of the funds he retained, he managed Ithaca without many visual changes to their
way of life. Then came WWII and more men left to
serve in uniforms. The woman that remained tried
to keep going but through the first 30 years of the
20th century, many of the craftsmen moved on, so
the little cottage shops no longer created a variety of
Ithaca products. The prolonged nature of the war
fallowed many of the fields, as there was no one to
work them. Many of the men did not return as they
fell in battles in Europe and the South Sea Islands.
Harry Dobbs body was sent back to his wife Jean.
She buried him by the chapel and Rev. Barton said
the words over him as a handful of villagers gathered around. The Japanese held Shem Tullane as a
prisoner of war. He was skin and bones when he

made it home, but everyone pitched in to do what was needed to nurse him back to health in body, though his mind always kept a closed off view of what he had endured. With the end of the war slowly others moved off for greener pastures in the cities as jobs in the factories paid them more than work at Ithaca could. The Wilson's faced what many of the great houses of the old world did. Their upstairs, downstairs and village families were leaving. They couldn't keep them there. Only the oldest remained living out their lives in familiar surroundings enjoying occasional letters and visits from children, grandchildren and friends.

Thankfully, Theodore had once again saw opportunities during WWII and the 1950s for industrial investments, and his choices allowed the Wilson's to garner enough money to survive even without Ithaca sustaining any major revenue. The village was blessed with no draftees during the Korean War. Ithaca Village in modern day is much like the big house, with areas closed up and unused. The mills, shops, the tavern, the chapel all sit empty. Only a handful of the cottages remain occupied by worker families, the Swansons – Elihue and Martha. Elihue helps with grounds keeping along with young Eval Patton and Lester Frank, Martha and Lester's wife Minnie, help with the house. Eval stayed after his father Eton passed away caring for all the remaining livestock and supporting Elihue. Brothers Hal and Otis Turnipton look after the buildings in the village and the big house, which always seem to need some mending. All these folks carry on the tradition as best they can like their folks before them. The financial investments from the Wilson's have kept everyone going. Every bill paid. Every need met. Now fifty years on since the deaths of Theodore and Margaret Wilson in the 1970s, the estate managed extremely well, but the money is running thin. Some things are put off for better times. The better times may not return for Ithaca. The Lady of the Manor carries on for all of them. All of them are a bit out of step with today, but quite happy in their stride.

"Ithaca's Legacy"

Ithaca Kitchen

Chapter Three

It's the worn wood boards, shiny marble floors, dirt and stone paths of Ithaca where Miss Allie Mae Wilson's immaculately shined shoes were most at home. It was in her kitchen where she left her footprints most evident.

The early-morning sun streamed in through the expansive windows of the Ithaca kitchen, filling the room with warm, golden light. At the Hoosier cabinet, the slender hands of the Lady of the Manor, Miss Allie, delicately arranged freshly baked blackberry muffins into a wicker basket.

As her hand crosses the wicker basket, it seems the wrinkles fade away to smoothness.

A smooth hand is pulling back from a wicker bassinet with a child wrapped in a blanket, which she places in the arms of her mother.

On an early morning in June of 1940, the only daughter of Theodore and Margaret Wilson came into the world with the aide of Dr. Elias Thaxton and was placed there for the first time by nurse Emily Jo Ames.

Rosy light filtered into the master bedroom of the manor, falling across the canopied bed where Margaret rested after hours of arduous labor. Her chestnut hair damp with perspiration, Margaret's petite figure seemed swallowed up amidst the mounds of

35

Ithaca Bedroom

down pillows and voluminous quilts. Her fair skin looked pale and wan, though her green eyes shone with a weary but euphoric joy.

At that moment, the bedroom door opened and Theodore entered, his towering silhouette filling the doorway. Quickly crossing the room in three long strides, his polished leather boots trod lightly on the Oriental rug as if remembering his sleeping wife. Theodore's strong jaw and piercing blue eyes were etched with emotion as he gazed down at the tightly wrapped bundle cradled in Margaret's arms – their newborn daughter. Reaching out a steady hand, Theodore gently swept back the lace edge of the receiving blanket to reveal their baby's face, flushed pink and dreaming, for the very first time.

Though years had weathered his tall, broad-shouldered frame, in this tender moment Theodore's upright posture radiated a father's pride. His neat mustache could not hide the smile tugging at the corners of his mouth beneath eyes glistening with joyful tears. Margaret beamed radiantly up at her husband, her cheery blush the only color in her wan cheeks. Together in awed silence they marveled at the tiny life they had brought into this world.

As she took her first breaths, the distant chimes of the chapel bells welcomed the newest heir to the Wilson legacy at Ithaca. Against the now open door leaned her older brother Liam, 17, as her father rushed to Margie's side. From Allie's nursery window, she could see for miles across fertile fields that made up the grounds of her family's land.

Allie's childhood unfolded within the sheltered confines of Ithaca, safe from the growing troubles of the outside world. Her playmates were the children of Ithaca's loyal workers.

The drumbeats of war were hidden largely from Allie, except for overhearing an occasional radio report as the family gathered in the parlor room in the evenings, or trying to understand as the fathers of some of her playmates left the farm to serve as volunteers or draftees. She was only one and a half when the Japanese bombed Pearl Harbor in 1941, and the fighting reached America's shores.

Though Theodore had managed to keep his son Liam well occupied helping run operations, his contemporaries were chiding him for not volunteering to serve.

One evening Allie was playing on the floor in the parlor, nineteen-year-old Liam Wilson bounded down the grand staircase of the manor, taking the steps two at a time. Tall and broad-shouldered like his father, Liam had the same piercing blue eyes and strong familial jaw line that hinted at the Wilsons' Irish roots. His thick dark hair, rumpled from sleep, fell roguishly over his forehead. His eager smile revealed a flash of white teeth as he entered the dining room.

Liam's youthful energy filled the room. He strode with purpose, his long, lean legs covering the Oriental rug in a few quick strides. As he sat down in the carved mahogany chair, Liam came in to tell his parent's that he had volunteered for the Marines and would be shipping out in two weeks.

Allie really didn't understand why her "Lem" was leaving, and she nearly choked him as she hung tightly about his neck saying goodbye with tears streaming down her face.

The village had banded together with the nearby Henton to support the war effort. Allie grew watching all the young men depart one by one until the fields stood empty. Those left behind took on added responsibilities.

As she grew, she became a daddy's girl, tagging along for fishing and hunting trips, leaning more towards being a tomboy than engaging in childhood tea parties and parlor games. She played hide-and-seek amid the veil of Spanish moss in the old oak grove, and staged elaborate plays on the sweeping front lawn with the other kids as players and all the adults as the audience.

On lazy summer days, Allie would sneak into the kitchen to pilfer cookies fresh from the oven baked by Esther, their portly cook. Despite always having fun at her hand, when the work of Ithaca was at hand, she was trained in all the aspects of what to do.

When the September cotton harvest arrived, Allie joined the crews dragging their burlap sacks through the fields, sticky puffs of cotton clinging to her dress as she labored alongside her friends.

Often, on Wednesday summer nights; Allie would fall asleep to the rhythm of hymns being sung in the chapel drifting through her open window. The chapel rested at the heart of their close-knit community, binding them together and giving them hope, as the war seemed endless. Allie alongside the women all hoped and prayed for the safe return of the boys across the sea.

"Ithaca's Legacy"

In 1944, a black bicycle from Henton arrived at the gate; it was George Thompson, the delivery boy from the Western Union office. He road up kicked the stand and went up on the portico. He knocked.

The heavy mahogany door of Ithaca swung open, revealing Joshua, standing tall in the entryway. His ebony skin glowed reflecting the outdoors, contrasting crispily with the white gloves encasing his large hands and starched white jacket of his butler's uniform. Though only twenty-eight, Joshua carried himself with a dignified grace that belied his years.

His muscular frame nearly filled the doorway, having inherited the imposing height and broad shoulders of the generations of men in his family who served at Ithaca. Joshua's posture was rigidly upright, shoulders back in proper form as a servant of the manor. His chiseled features held high cheekbones and a strong jaw line that would have appeared stern if not for the warmth in his brown eyes.

Joshua's thick black hair was trimmed neat and tidy. As he reached out to accept the telegram from the messenger, the gold band on his left ring finger glinted, signaling his recent marriage to his childhood sweetheart.

"Telegraph for the Wilson's sir, from the war department," George said. Joshua took it, giving George a generous half dollar from his pocket, and placing the telegram on a silver tray with his white-gloved hand. He carried it into the dining room as the family was gathered for dinner.

He held the plate out to Theodore, as Margie caught a glimpse of it being a telegram. She knew what it might mean. She rose holding her napkin to her face as she walked towards the window.

Theodore opened it discovering the dreadful news – Liam had perished in a bloody battle following the D Day landing at Normandy.

He laid the telegram back on the silver tray, walked over to Margie, put his arms around her and held her tightly as she began to cry and fell into his arms not able to hold her own weight.

Allie seeing what was happening, not understanding, joined them wrapping her little arms around their legs as she wept bitter tears too. When what happened was eventually explained to her, the loss left an ache inside her young heart.

With each passing year, Margie guided Allie into her role as a gentile young lady. With the death of Liam, she was now the elder child, and someday, she would be in charge of Ithaca. She brought in dance tutors, language tutors, riding instructors, in anticipation of sending her to the Magnolia Finishing School when she reached the age of 12.

Her training was sidelined a bit in her ninth year, when her parents were surprised with the news that there was another child on the way. They both worried, as Margie was 43. Margie did manage to keep some attention on Allie as the pregnancy grew on her.

Despite her best efforts though, Allie was more at home working in the fields or fishing or swimming with the other village children. Despite the daytime activity, Margie insisted she was with them in the evenings as they sat on their Ithaca porch watching the fireflies dance across the fields. Sometimes she

Allie in the Cotton Field

would slip away, saying I'm going to bed, only to quietly embark down the back stairs, slip out the back door and head down to the village, where she would sit outside listening to the women gossip as the men sat in the tavern and the fiddler sawed reels.

On Saturday nights, the family and the villagers attended socials and box suppers where there was music and dancing.

In about six months, Margie gave birth to Charles John Wilson. Allie was elated to see her new younger brother. To add to the joy, the family butler Joshua and his wife Myra also welcomed a new son that they named Craven. So, two young boys would soon have the run of Ithaca and growing up side by side.

Allie soon blossomed into a beautiful and charming belle of sixteen as America eased into the age of Rock and Roll, though at Ithaca, the modern sounds were as foreign as life in Tibet. The world ahead seemed bright with promise, as the young men of Henton were very smitten with young Allie.

Her coming out at the Magnolia Debutante Ball in Jackson was a tremendous success and she soon had suitors calling on her from throughout the region.

She was in no hurry though as college was in her plans and she had to prepare for all her future

Magnolia Debutante Ball

responsibilities of running the estate.

One of the young men she met at her debutante ball did not forget her though. His shyness precluded him from asking her to dance or even calling upon her at Ithaca.

Allie knelt on the concrete walkway, hurriedly gathering up the textbooks and papers strewn around her. In her rush across campus, she had collided with another student coming around the corner, sending them both tumbling in a flurry of loose leaf and literature. As Allie reached for the last American Literature anthology, a strong hand grasped it first and extended it down to her. She lifted her gaze and found herself staring into the kindest hazel eyes she had ever seen.

David Turner stood tall above her. His tousled chestnut hair shone golden in the light, framing his handsome, boyish face. One corner of his mouth ticked up in a crooked grin as he helped Allie to her feet. David had shot up over six feet since he first saw her at her debutante ball. Now 21 years old, his shoulders had broadened into an athletic physique to fill out his cotton button-down and khaki trousers.

Allie's heart quickened as she steadied herself with David's sturdy grip.

As they knelt again gathering the disarray of books, Allie's blue eyes lifted to meet David's warm hazel gaze once more. In that moment, something passed between them – a spark of undeniable connection. Allie knew then that this chance encounter had changed the trajectory of their futures forever. They soon found themselves dating and as graduation neared in 1962, David asked Allie to marry. Of course, he still had to get permission from Theodore, she reminded him. But if he agreed, she would also.

So, a trip back to Ithaca was planned. However, before the trip was made, a letter came for David with greetings from the United States.

He was being drafted for service in the Air Force.

He had already served in the ROTC and had been taking training as a pilot.

This curve was not expected in their plans and with him being away for a couple of years was unsure whether to go ahead.

He decided to talk with Theodore about the whole situation. He kept David sweating and fidgeting in his shoes, but he eventually agreed to the marriage suggesting that they wait for his return from Vietnam.

David didn't really want to wait, but understood and agreed to his terms. Allie was not pleased but the two men in her life had made a decision she had to live with, so she waited.

After their parting, Allie had returned to Ithaca to help her father alongside her brother now calls Johnny, who was now a teenager himself. Allie spent each day dreading the possibility of a telegram arriving like it had for her brother.

One morning in 1964, Allie stood silent and numb as not a telegram but an Air Force captain whose name is lost in the moment. He informed her that David's fighter had been shot down during a mission over the jungle. He was not an official envoy as they had gone to David's parents. The captain was one of David's buddies who had promised he would deliver a letter to her. There was no body to bury, no goodbye to find closure. Just some loving

Allie receives news about David.

words scribbled on paper. Her beloved was just gone, leaving her alone with a broken heart at twenty-four.

Allie's heart simply closed as she enveloped herself in the business of Ithaca.

The seasons, the plantings, the harvests passed one by one. With each passing year Theodore, Margie, Allie and Johnny grew closer and closer.

Johnny wasted no time in finding whom he wanted to spend his life with. It was an unexpected meeting when he had gone to Henton.

He shoved his hands in his pockets as he left the Open Door Cafe. As his eyes adjusted, they fell upon a vision standing just down the sidewalk. A girl about his age was peering in a window, her willowy silhouette backlit. As she turned, Johnny's breath caught in his throat.

Michelle Armstrong had creamy tan skin that glowed in the warm light. Her raven hair cascaded over her shoulders in loose curls, framing her oval face. She had accented cheekbones, full lips, and lively espresso-colored eyes lined with long lashes.

Michelle wore a fitted orange and white striped tee shirt tucked into hip hugging bell-bottoms, accentuating her slender curves. Multiple beaded necklaces from the Jackson art fair danced above her fringe vest. On her feet were brown leather glad-iator sandals that laced up her calves.

As Michelle noticed Johnny, she flashed a bril-liant smile that hit him like a lightning bolt. In that moment, the outside world faded away and all John-ny saw was she. He was utterly enraptured by this cosmopolitan girl from the big city. Johnny knew then and there that his heart belonged to this beauti-ful vision before him.

She was traveling with her parents who had got-ten off the bus and were eating at the diner. She had already finished and was looking around the town. Never a timid one, he introduced himself saying I want to marry you. She smiled and they talked. She soon was back on the Greyhound with her folks headed to Jackson leaving her number on a torn piece of notebook paper in Johnny's pocket.

The very next weekend he found a reason to go to Jackson and it wasn't long before he and she eloped leaving no room for either set of parents to interfere in their plans.

Needless to say Theodore and Margie were incensed that their young son would be so impetuous. Allie was a bit more understanding remembering her missed opportunity with David. Johnny brought her back to Ithaca, but not to move in, just to inform the family that he and Michelle would be moving to Memphis where the two of them would be starting a new path.

Letters and calls from the couple were few and far between, except for the news that Michelle was pregnant, then the news that Johnny had been drafted and was going to Vietnam. He was already gone when their little boy Alan Wilson was born. One day, Michelle called and told Allie that Johnny was killed in Vietnam. Allie begged Michelle to come and live at Ithaca, but she didn't. Word eventually reached the family that she had remarried and moved west and was living in a commune.

As the seventies ticked by, Ithaca found it harder and harder to be successful in any of its endeavors. They attended Sunday services without fail, finding peace in the familiar rituals even with loved ones now absent from the worn pews. Allie took over managing the household full-time as Margaret's health declined. Margie was the first to take her place in the shady cemetery by the chapel. She was broken hearted at the loss of her sons to wars she did not even understand. Her health declined quickly though Allie and Theodore did all they could. Her heart just gave out.

Theodore was not far behind her as a cancer of the lungs came upon him. They lay side by side in the Wilson family plot.

Though Allie inherited Ithaca, the empty halls only magnified her loneliness. She found herself clinging to tradition to keep her footing, even as the world changed rapidly around her.

Craven, now a man of 27 had missed out on the draft and was still working at Ithaca. It fell to him to hang the painting of Miss Allie over the fireplace in the parlor, replacing that of Theodore and moving him to the hall with his forefathers. Miss Allie was now the Lady of the Manor. It was up to her to forge the future.

Somehow despite the grief, Allie found the strength to carry on. She focused on Ithaca. She oversaw the operations and its remaining workers with a dignified efficiency like the Lady of the Manor she was bred to be. The work kept her busy, though solitary. Allie witnessed the steady decline of the Southern way of life she held so dear. The village craftsmen shops sat empty, their trades now lost to time. Gaps marred the chapel pews where generations of faithful souls once sat. Weeds overtook the outlying fields with no hands left to tend the acreage.

An occasional letter would let her know of Michelle and Alan's progress, then those just stopped. Allie tried to find them but to no avail. More than twenty years passed, then one day a black Cadillac pulled up in front of Ithaca. An appointment had been set with Miss Allie by phone. The man getting out of the car came to the door, knocked, and waited.

The heavy mahogany door swung open to reveal a tall, distinguished gentleman in a tailored gray suit. He stood with perfect posture; one hand holding a leather briefcase while the other adjusted his thin silver glasses. His salt-and-pepper hair was neatly parted and combed. As he stepped inside, his polished Oxfords clicked crisply on the marble floors.

This was Thomas Acres, a lawyer from Fresno. His angular features held an air of somber duty, from the sharp line of his jaw to the furrow between his brows. His piercing icy green eyes surveyed the foyer, glinting with intelligence. With his tall, lean frame clad impeccably in his pressed suit and tie, James cut an imposing figure.

He presented his card softening his stern expression into a polite smile to Craven, who showed him to the parlor. There he awaited Miss Allie.

When she entered, though James bore grievous news, he stood and he soon got to business.

"Miss Wilson, I am here to settle the estate of Alan and Gloria Wilson," he said.

"Estate?" she questioned.

"Yes, your nephew and his wife were killed in an auto accident in Fresno, California two weeks ago," he said.

Keeping her composure, she fought to hold back tears for a nephew she had never seen except in a mailed childhood photo.

"This is sad news, what am I to do to help?" she inquired.

"Well, the reason I am hear so quickly, is they left everything they had to their four-year-old son Asbury Jesse Wilson, and they left he and his care to you," he said. "Here is all the paperwork. They didn't leave much financially, mainly life insurance settlements. That is all here. I have him at the hotel with a nurse and I would like to bring him here as soon as possible."

Allie's face changed from the near crying to joy as she thought of having a nephew to come and grow up at Ithaca.

"Bring him. Nonsense, we are coming with you to get him." she exclaims. She then called loudly,

"Craven, bring the car, we are headed to Henton to bring our nephew home."

She rushed to the kitchen picked up a wicker basket she had just filled with muffins, thinking that may be something her new nephew would like and it might break the ice of the situational meeting.

Miss Allie found a new reason to strive for the future success of her beloved Ithaca. There was another generation to provide for and no matter how much she loved her adopted family members; Ithaca would have another Wilson at its helm one day.

The years passed, a new millennium came to Henton and Jesse grew into an amazing young man through the first two decades of the 21st Century. He moved to Henton in 2012 to gain some independence, married Suzy Hendrix, a girl he met at college, soon after. They began a family with their son Jake. Sadly, Suzy died of a hereditary blood disease when Jake was about one and a half leaving Jesse to raise him on his own. He checked on Allie daily and assisted however he could, to show a kinship and shared reverence for their family legacy. She came to think of him almost as a son. Miss Allie took pride in Jesse entering the police academy, the first of the Wilsons to serve Henton in that capacity. She attended his graduation full of beaming smiles.

In 2005, the town held a grand celebration to

honor Allie's 65 years as the Lady of Ithaca. She rode in the parade wearing a splendid day dress and hat, waving to familiar faces from the manor house's antique Rolls Royce. The townspeople showed their abiding love for the grand dame who worked tirelessly to preserve their way of life.

Miss Allie's wrinkled hand places one last muffin in the wicker basket, raises it and drops it at her side. At eighty years old, Miss Allie still carries herself with the poise and elegance of Southern gentility, her petite frame draped in a floral day dress. Her snow-white hair is perfectly coiffed and her wise blue eyes speak of her prestigious lineage.

Humming softly to herself "Nearer My God to Thee," Miss Allie sets the basket aside and unties her apron, draping the flour-dusted linen over a chair. She smoothes the fabric of her dress, an antiquated style more suited for the 1930s than the 21st century. But high fashion matters little to Miss Allie these days.

"Craven, have you got the car ready?" she calls, her voice thin but firm. When no reply comes, Miss Allie lifts the basket and made her way through the manor's grand foyer towards the front door.

The halls stood quiet save the ticking of clocks like a heartbeat. In many rooms, sheets shrouded the furniture in a ghostly hush. The finery of decades past is tarnished to a lusterless sheen.

Southern Crossing

She passes detailed paintings of stern-faced ancestors staring down from the wallpapered walls. There is William, William Jr., James, Daniel – the Revolutionary War hero, Daniel Jr., and Charles in his Confederate uniform, Andrew, and Theodore. Out on the portico, the morning sunlight glints off the polished burgundy hood of a 1924 Rolls-Royce Silver Ghost touring car. Outside, the elements had weathered Ithaca's formerly majestic façade.

At the vehicle's side stood Craven Wilson, his salt-and-pepper hair peeks out from beneath his driver's cap.

Though decades had weathered his tall, slender frame, Craven's warm brown eyes hold a lively spirit. When Craven started working at the big house, he was valet-in-training for Miss Allie's father and brothers. He learned all about running the household from his father Joshua. Eventually, one-by-one the valets, chauffer, upstairs and downstairs maids, cook, servers and the rest gave way to changes of time. But Craven, always the perfect butler tries to fill as many roles as he can. As he notices Miss Allie's approach, he ceases polishing the Ghost's elegant chrome and teak accents and turns to her with a smile.

"Miss Allie, where are we headed today?" he asks in his gentle baritone.

Craven walks around to open the Ghost's rear

passenger door, the luxurious leather and wood interior awaiting its matriarchal passenger.

The duo then aims the Ghost through the Ithaca arch toward Henton.

The small town of Henton, Mississippi rests in a gentle valley northeast of the capital city of Jackson.

Henton, Mississippi

Though the 21st century continues on around it, within Henton's borders it seems time has stopped somewhere in the early 1900s.

The town center is anchored by a stately courthouse built in the early 1800s with imposing columns and a clock tower looming over the main square where a statue of Major Wilson stands watch over the town.

Inside, the polished marble floors and intricately carved wooden doors harkens back to a more genteel era. Just off the square, brick storefronts house local shops and cafes, their once vibrant painted signs faded from decades of Southern sun.

The streets are lined with 1970s pickup trucks. Even an occasional horse-drawn buggy is still a common sight.

Many of the two-lane roads outside of town are simply graded dirt, laid decades before asphalt became the norm. And while power lines connect the homes, modern conveniences are at a minimum.

The wood-frame houses surrounding downtown are straight out of the turn of the 20th century, with wide porches and belching chimneys.

Gas lamps cast faint halos of light along the streets at night. The technology around town is an eclectic mix of 19th and early 20th century, from the operator-connected landline phones to the printing presses churning out the weekly newspaper.

Though just a short drive from Jackson, visiting Henton feels like entering a different world. The pace of life moves slower, without the urgent rush of the modern age.

What made Henton the island of antiquity it is? The towns and cities nearby exploded in growth in the good times as every technological advance became commonplace. Their populations grew. But

Boss Henton, his father and grandfather before him who ran the county and the city since Reconstruction as their personal kingdom. They held a tight grip while running the county allowing only what they liked, and what benefited them and their web of lackeys who they kept in power in every office or job of influence or control. While the last Henton had shook off his mortal coil, their interests were slow in fading. Of those they put in power, many remained and over the years, the residents actually grew fond of the eclectic mix of old and new the Hentons solidified. Rather than pushing for advancement and change, the people held on strongly to what was, and did all they could to overt the future from interfering in their lives. But Henton was changing. New people were finding their way into the offices of power and influence and wanting to shape the future to their liking no matter what or who stood in their way.

However, the friendly, familiar community of Henton values tradition and preserving a way of life from a simpler time gone by. So, the infusion of new people and ideas became a tug-of-war within its confines. The majority of people felt the 21st century shouldn't infringe upon Henton's treasured past. But no one will go untouched by these struggles.

"Ithaca's Legacy"

Henton Courthouse

Chapter Four

On the old courthouse's second and third floors wood-paneled hallways exude the musty charm of a bygone era. Chief Randolph Wayne's boots click against the creaking floorboards as he makes his way past the various second floor office doors, each bearing an engraved nameplate harkening back to the days of Boss Henton's ironclad rule.

At the entrance to the Tax Commissioner's office, Horace Rigson emerges just as the Chief approaches. Rigson was a slender, spectacled man with a deferential manner about him.

"Hello Horace how's your mama and them?" Wayne asks in his gravelly baritone.

"Fine, Chief – how's the crime rate?" Rigson replies politely. "Going down, unlike our taxes," Wayne quips with a wry smile.

Rigson let out an obliging chuckle before scurrying off down the hall. Shaking his head, the Chief continues on until he reaches the office of the County Planning Commissioner.

Upon entering the spacious corner office, Wayne finds Commissioner George Hargrove, a portly, jovial man, enthusiastically pumping the hand of a sharply dressed stranger—clearly the big-city developer he had heard about. The developer, James Harris, is tall and lean, with slicked-back hair and an arrogant glint in his eye.

"Gentlemen," Wayne announces gruffly by way of greeting. "Mornin' Chief," Hargrove replies breezily. "This is James Harris, the land developer who wants to build a new shopping center near Henton."

Wayne shook the proffered hand while giving a skeptical once-over.

After taking a seat, Hargrove explains his request for Wayne to introduce Harris to the owners of the proposed development site. When prompted, Harris eagerly shows Wayne the location on a framed map hanging on the wall.

"George, who owns the property?" Wayne asks with a furrowed brow.

"The smaller lots belong to Howard Moses and Billy Sherrill," Hargrove explains. "The larger parcel is owned by a Miss Wilson."

Wayne stiffens at the familiar name. "Miss Allie Mae Wilson?"

"Yes, that's her," confirms Hargrove.

Wayne leans back in his chair, lips pursing beneath his graying mustache. "Yeah well, I'll go with you in the morning and introduce you around, but I don't think you'll have any luck with Miss Wilson."

Despite the warning, Harris maintains his slick, confident demeanor. "Thank you Chief Wayne. We'll talk to her about it. I'm staying at the Suns

Motel – should I meet you?"

"No, I'll pick you up about nine," Wayne replies gruffly, already dreading the task at hand.

After exchanging terse handshakes, the men part ways, leaving Harris to contemplate just how he would charm the resistant Miss Wilson.

As Wayne's worn cowboy boots clomp down the hallway, echoing off the antique wainscoting lining the walls. His heels cross the elaborate diamond design cast by dusty beams of light shining form the windows on the creaking wooden floors.

While the Boss system was long gone from Henton, Wayne was the closest to it and he aims to uphold that frontier justice in his little corner of the world.

As the Chief strode past the row of engraved office doors, Councilman Bob Evers emerges from around a corner. The young politician exuded big-city energy, from his stylish suit to his confident grin.

"Chief, I was hoping to see you," Evers greets Wayne cheerily.

Wayne glowers beneath the brim of his Stetson hat.

"Well, how is our resident Yankee Carpetbagger this morning?" he grumbles.

Unfazed, Evers flashes his pearly white smile.

"Chief, if I didn't know you better I would think you didn't like me."

Wayne stares back stonily, his craggy face unmoving.

Oblivious to the Chief's scorn, Evers prattles on.

"Yes, well, I want you to know the officer we hired from Washington will be in today. I want you to make her welcome."

At this, Wayne bristles, his bushy gray mustache twitching. "It's bad enough you want me to bring in some hippy from the city. Why did it have to be a black woman?"

"They're called African-Americans now, Chief," Evers corrects gently.

"It's taken me this long to call them black!" Wayne snaps. "I could have hired from town, somebody like Elsi Watkin's boy. He would understand how things are in Henton with his folks. He wouldn't be coming here with all those liberal hippy ideas...and all that new-fangled police education which can only cause more problems."

Undeterred, Evers flashes his politician's smile. "Change is good, Chief."

Wayne's craggy face curls into a sneer. "Only when you're using a remote; and I think I've seen enough of this show."

With that, the Chief turns on his worn heel and strode away down the creaking hallway. Evers' voice echoes after him, "African-American, Chief!"

"Ithaca's Legacy"

Henton Police Department

Chapter Five

The humid Southern air hung heavy as the vintage Rolls-Royce Silver Ghost glided to a stop at the curb outside the police station, its burgundy finish ignoring the faded stripes of the parking spaces. Craven hurries around the side of the classic sedan to open the passenger door.

"Thank you, Craven. I'll just be a minute," says Miss Allie as she steps gingerly onto the sidewalk. The woman moves with the grace of old Southern gentility as she picks up her basket and breezes up the steps to the station.

Just inside the station door, the hulking frame of Officer B.J. 'Bear' Bryson hunches over paperwork at the long, green-and-yellow wooden front counter. Bear's meaty hands made the forms look tiny as he scribbles notes. Nearby at another desk, the pudgy Officer Jimmy Ellison shuffles papers; his round boyish face scrunches in concentration. When Miss Allie enters, the clacking of typewriters and shuffling of feet stops abruptly as all eyes turn to the elderly woman.

The officers straighten their posture or rise up respectfully to their feet.

"Hello, boys," Miss Allie greets warmly. "Where's my nephew Jesse?" She scans the crowded squad room, which housed about a half a dozen desks but did not spot the familiar face. Jimmy offers to fetch him from the back, his high voice polite despite his clumsy demeanor. As Miss Allie makes her way past the cluster of uniformed men, conversations resume in hushed tones.

At the end of the hall, she encounters Jesse emerging from the jail. Her lanky nephew looks so much like photos of his late father Alan, with his serious brow and gentle eyes, she thought as she saw him.

"Aunt Allie, what are you doing back here?" Jesse asks protectively, steering her back toward the front.

"You know it's blackberry time," Miss Allie replies, unveiling a basket of muffins. "I brought some muffins. Last year there wasn't a fit berry to be found."

At the sight and scent of Miss Allie's baking, the officers swarm around like bees to honey. Bear's meaty hands snatch a muffin as he lumbers back to the front counter.

Just then, the station doors swing open, and in bursts Sonja Hemings. Her outfit is more suited for the clubs of D.C. than the streets of small-town Henton.

She had taken one look at the parking spaces outside and bristled. "Someone's car is blocking all the parking spaces!" she announces in annoyance.

From the counter, Bear grumbles over his mouthful of muffin. "We know. It's Miss Allie..."

Before he could finish, Chief Wayne strode in, scans the room, and quietly asks Bear about Miss Allie's whereabouts. After getting his bearings, Wayne could see just a bit of her silver-white hair through the mass of his force and he made his way through the crowd toward Miss Allie and Jesse, but pauses at the sight of Sonja's irritation.

"Bear, see if you can help this girl. Looks like she needs it," Wayne mutters under his breath.

After politely extricating Miss Allie from the hub-bub, Chief Wayne requests she join him and Jesse in his office. As they step inside and close the door, the ruckus in the squad room erupts once more.

"Hey, you King Kong, are you going to help me or not?" Sonja yells at Bear.

All eyes turn to the source – a young black woman who stood defiantly, one hand cocked on her hip.

Jimmy hurries over, stammering nervously, "Little lady, I don't think you meant to raise your voice to Bear..."

Jimmy tries to calm the escalating situation, but Bear and Sonja continue trading barbs.

But Sonja is unfazed. "Are you threatening me, King Kong?" she challenges, glaring up at Bear's imposing form.

Bear holds up a hand. "I don't make threats," he rumbles.

Incensed, Sonja unleashes a tirade of insults, her voice rising to a shout. Just then, the office door bangs open and Chief Wayne storms out, face like a thundercloud.

"What the heck is going on out here?" Wayne bellows. "What's the problem, Bear?"

Bear shook his shaggy head wearily. "This young lady was just telling me what she thinks of me."

Wayne's eyes narrows beneath his graying brow

"Well, Miss, you're under arrest for disturbing the peace," he growls. "Jimmy, read her that thing and take her to the cells."

As Jimmy escorts the protesting Sonja away, she says, "But Chief, I'm here to see you."

Chief Wayne adds in response over his shoulder, "Well, now, we'll be seeing a lot of each other."

The office door slams shut behind him, leaving silence to settle once again across the station.

"Ithaca's Legacy"

Henton Police Department

Chapter Six

Chief Wayne's office in the Henton Police Department still holds the rustic charm of decades past. His wide oak desk was carved with ornate scrollwork fit for the stately manor homes of old Southern gentry. Sunlight filtering through the frosted glass transom casts an intimate glow across the well-worn leather chairs crowded into the cozy room.

There was a long settee upholstered with black leathers along the wall. Behind him on the wall were photos of chiefs past. On his desk was green glass shaded reading lamp, a desk calendar, and a phone. He had one other item on the desk, a little ceramic girl reclining on a lounge; its leg would kick in the air when prompted.

Seated across from Chief Wayne, Miss Allie perched tensely on the edge of her seat. Her petite frame held tall, accentuating the graceful poise of a true Southern belle. Beside her, Officer Jesse Wilson slouches in his chair, his lanky frame dwarfing the antique furniture.

"Miss Allie, what I want to speak to you about — ," Chief Wayne begins slowly.

But the elderly woman interrupts, her words spilling out in an anxious rush. "My, that young lady could use a good..."

73

"Switchin'?" Jesse offered wryly, raising one brow. Miss Allie purses her lips. "No, I was going to say finishing school. They would never allow such an outburst."

Chief Wayne clears his throat gruffly. "Yes, well, as I was saying, I just came from the County Planning Commissioner's office, and there's a land developer who wants to build a new shopping center near Henton."

"That's wonderful!" Miss Allie exclaims, clapping her gloved hands together. "You know, Jess, I told some of the ladies at the Southern Women's League just the other day we need a new notions store. Do you think there will be a notions store?"

The Chief shook his head. "Well, I don't know, but they want to build it out on the Confederate Highway."

"Near my home?" Miss Allie asks. Her smile fades.

"As a matter of fact, that's where they want to build – at Ithaca," Chief Wayne confirms grimly. "They want to buy it."

Miss Allie recoils as if struck, her face draining of color. "Buy Ithaca?" she whispers.

The Chief and Jesse exchange an uneasy glance as a heavy silence fell over the room.

Finally Miss Allie speaks, her voice tight with conviction: "The Yankees didn't even take Ithaca when they came through and they tried. No land developer is going to get it."

She rises swiftly, chin held high.

"Good day, Randolph," she adds with finality, taking Jesse's arm as she sweeps briskly from the office.

Open Door Cafe

Chapter Seven

A light breeze stirs the drooping branches of the magnolia trees surrounding the Henton Police Department, carrying their sweet floral scent through the sleepy town. As the carved oak door swung open, Miss Allie emerges into the afternoon light, raising a delicately gloved hand to shade her eyes.

At the curb, the polished burgundy hood of the vintage Rolls-Royce glints where the faithful friend Craven stands waiting beside the open rear door. His weathered face creases into a warm smile as Officer Jesse Wilson escorts his elderly aunt down the stone steps.

"Hello Crav, how are you?" Jesse asks.

"Fine, son, fine," Craven replies.

Miss Allie lifts her chin as she approaches the luxury sedan. "Craven, let's go over to the Open Door Cafe," she directs crisply. "Would you mind moving the car?"

"No ma'am, I'll be right in," Craven assures her.

Jesse glances both ways before guiding his aunt across the sleepy street; the breeze stirs the magnolias overhead. As Craven slides behind the wheel, he gently closes the door once he settles inside. Jesse and Miss Allie make their way toward the cozy cafe, its red gingham curtains beckoning them inside.

The cheerful jingle of the bell announces Jesse and Miss Allie's arrival at the Open Door Cafe. The cozy eatery is a cornerstone of the community; its worn oak floors and faded gingham tablecloths exude small-town charm. Behind the register, owner Pearly Mae Selby looks up from her ticket book, her warm smile creases the laugh lines around her eyes.

"Why Miss Allie, Jesse! How are you?" Pearly Mae greets.

Jesse's gaze swept over the busy restaurant. "Hey Aunt Pearl, where's Nate?"

"He's running around here somewhere," Pearly Mae replies with a knowing grin. Right on cue, five-year-old Nate barrels through the cafe, makeshift airplane in hand.

"Daddy, Daddy, see my new plane!" Nate cries.

He hugs his aunt and Craven before dashing off again, unable to contain his boundless energy.

From a corner table, Bob and Tess rise respectfully as Miss Allie enters.

Would you like this table, Miss Allie?" Bob asks in his gravelly drawl.

Bob is in his early sixties, a contemporary of Chief Wayne's. He's a local good ole boy, often seen around town wearing his trademark ensemble – faded blue bib overalls, a wrinkled plaid shirt, and a tattered John Deere cap perched atop his balding head. His favorite had carved pipe in the shape of a bearded fat faced fellow is always hanging out of the corner of his mouth, though he stopped smoking years earlier. While he comes across as a harmless town fixture, Bob has a mischievous sparkle in his eye and a knack for being less than honest when it suits him.

"Why thank you Bob, there are still southern gentlemen," Miss Allie replies warmly.

Tess fishes for a compliment as well, chirping, "Miss Allie, you look as fresh as dew on a morning glory!"

Tess is in her mid-fifties and runs the local beauty parlor called "The Henton Rinse." She has big blonde hair styled in a dramatic 1960s bouffant and wears a brightly colored dress straight from the fashion runways of Paris in 1967. Tess knows everyone in town and makes it her business to know their business too. She's seen every head in Henton come through her salon chairs over the years and delights in passing along any rumor or tidbit of gossip she hears. With her chatty nature and affinity for drama, Tess keeps a steady stream of town talk flowing through "The Henton Rinse."

Miss Allie pauses, considering her response.

"Sometimes I wonder, Tess," she murmurs cryptically, eliciting a flummoxed look from the beautician.

Miss Allie's gaze grew distant. "Jesse, I don't

know about this land deal," she says, her brows knitting with concern.

In the nearest booth, a lone man looks up from his newspaper, his interest piqued by the conversation. James Harris found his mark. Keeping his head down, he continues listening to the Southern gentlewoman, who held the fate of his newest development in her gracious hands.

The clatter of dishes and aroma of sizzling food fills the cozy confines of the Open Door Cafe. Jesse pulls out a chair at an empty table and Miss Allie smoothed her dress before settling gracefully into the seat. Nearby, young Nate waves his makeshift airplane enthusiastically at his father.

"See you tonight," Jesse tells his energetic son. "Don't drive Aunt Pearl crazy."

"Yes sir!" Nate replies with a salute, and then scampers off to resume his adventures as Craven arrives.

Pearly Mae bustles over, order pad in hand. "What would you like today?"

"I'd like your special," Miss Allie requests politely.

Jesse and Craven quickly chime in with matching orders. As Pearly Mae shuffles off to the kitchen, a pensive look clouds Miss Allie's delicate features.

"Jesse, I just don't know," she murmurs. She went on to explain Chief Wayne's news about the bid for Ithaca to Craven, her gracious Southern lilt tinged with worry.

James Harris continues eavesdropping with keen interest as the trio at the table reminisces fondly about growing up at Ithaca.

"It is your home, yours, mine, Jesse's, and some-day Nate's, and all the folks who still are at the village," Craven implores passionately. "But Miss Allie, there would be a lot of money involved."

Jesse reaches across to grasp their hands reassuringly.

"This decision is yours," he says supportively. "If you're both happy, then I will be."

Miss Allie lifts her chin. "I couldn't be happy anywhere but Ithaca," she declares with steely conviction.

At this, Harris tosses his newspaper aside and strides over to their table. "Excuse me, Miss Wilson, I'm James Harris," he interjects smoothly. "I was hoping you might join me to discuss your land."

Miss Allie recoils at the intrusion. "I don't believe I'm interested in speaking with you right now," she rebuffs icily.

But Harris persists, ignoring Jesse's rising protests. As he crowds Miss Allie's space, Jesse shoots up from his seat. "Now look, Harris —" he begins heatedly.

Harris brusquely shoves Jesse aside. Incensed,

"Ithaca's Legacy"

Jesse rears back, fist clenched and cocked — as Chief Wayne appears in the doorway. "Jesse!" Wayne exclaims in surprise. The room falls silent, all eyes locked on the brewing confrontation.

"Ithaca's Legacy"

Henton Police Department

Chapter Eight

Jesse Wilson sat at his desk in the Henton Police Department squad room, reviewing case files and nursing a piping-hot cup of coffee. The stale scent of old paperwork and worn furniture permeates the aged walls of the precinct.

Jimmy Ellison strolls up to the desk across from him. Jimmy's wide grin and upbeat energy contrast the otherwise sleepy atmosphere.

"Jesse, your aunt is a unique lady," Jimmy says, leaning against the desk.

Jesse smiles, pride for his Southern roots evident on his face. "She's a real Southern belle."

"I heard there's gold all over her place," Jimmy adds, raising his eyebrows.

At that moment, Officer Bear Bryson looks up from the front desk where he is working. Bear turns and walks over to join the conversation, his heavy boots thudding on the tile floor.

"There's that legend again," Bear chimes in, shaking his head. His gruff voice rumbles through the room.

"No, not that again," Jesse sighs, having grown tired of this tall tale over the years.

"What legend is that?" Jimmy asks, intrigued.

Bear eagerly launches into the dramatic story.

"Jesse's great, great, great grandfather was paymaster general of the western Confederate army. In the last days before the fall of Vicksburg, he was killed by Grant's forces." Bear pauses for effect. "They say he was storing the gold the night he was killed at Ithaca."

"Man," Jimmy exhales, picturing the scene vividly.

"That's not all, is it, Bear?" Jesse prods irritably.

Chief Wayne suddenly emerges from his office and steps into the squad room.

"Are you planning to work today or would you like me to put in a pot-bellied stove and cracker barrel so you can play checkers and chew the fat?" Chief Wayne bellows.

Everyone scrambles back to work, avoiding eye contact.

"That's just great," Chief Wayne, grumbles, clearly having overheard them. "Bear, why don't you go get Ms. Hemings and bring her to my office...and be nice."

Wayne shoots Jimmy a pointed look. "After I talk with her, I've got some news for all of you."

Bear takes off while Chief Wayne turns to Jesse.

"Jesse, I'm supposed to bring that Harris character out to your aunt's place around noon tomorrow. I want you there and I want you to remember you're a police officer. Leave your boxing gloves at home," he says.

"Yes sir, Chief. I'll be there...without my gloves," Jesse acquiesces.

Chief Wayne turns to Jimmy, "Tell me about the girl."

"Well, all she would tell me was her name and where she's from – Washington," Jimmy explains.

"Washington, that figured," Chief Wayne grumbles from his office doorway, clearly eavesdropping.

"She's from Washington DC," Jimmy clarifies.

"Washington, eh? Her name Hemings?" Wayne asks.

Jimmy shook his head as Bear escorts the woman directly into the chief's office without saying another word. He sat her down in the chair facing the chief's desk.

"Jimmy, what did you get on our female guest?" Wayne asks.

Jimmy hands him a file and follows Chief Wayne back into his office, where Sonja Hemings already sits waiting. Jimmy moves to stand guard near the door.

"That will be all, Jimmy, Bear" Chief Wayne orders gruffly.

"But Chief, rules require..." Jimmy begins to protest.

"Jimmy," Wayne interrupts sternly.

"Yes, sir," Jimmy acquiesces, both officers exiting and closing the door behind them.

Jesse studies the closed office door, pondering the mysterious visitor. Who is this Sonja Hemings and what did she want with their small town police force?

Bear eagerly resumes his dramatic legend. "No, they never did find the gold, but the ledger he kept was found on him. After the war, the Yankees showed it to General Pemberton, he acted like he couldn't read it, but years later he said to his family it showed over half a million in gold had been counted." His voice drops low. "Everyone thinks Wilson's family has it hidden away."

Jesse rolls his eyes in exasperation. Some tales never seem to die.

Chief Wayne turns his attention to the striking woman before him.

"Miss Hemings, I presume?"

"Yes, Chief," she replies evenly.

Leaning back in his worn leather chair, Wayne eyes her critically. "Miss Hemings, what do you have to say for yourself?"

Sonja bristles at his accusatory tone. "Me...I didn't do anything."

"Oh, I see," Wayne, continues sharply. "You just like to start a new job by alienating all officers in the department by charging at them like a wild boar."

Sonja met his glare defiantly. "Officers? All that

is out there is a Klan meeting in blue."

Chief Wayne's face reddens at the insult to his men. "Miss Hemings, you may not like those men, but if I'm going up against somebody shooting at me, out of their head on somethin', I'd rather have one of them covering my back than a hot head like you."

Sonja leans forward, unwilling to back down.

"Chief, I'm a good officer. I was top of my class at the academy," she exclaims.

"I am aware of that, Miss Hemings," Chief Wayne admits begrudgingly. "I am also aware from my old friend the Commander at the Academy, that you were the most disciplined cadet that they ever had, and it looks like it didn't faze you in the least."

He pauses, considering her with a mixture of irritation and grudging respect.

"You know, I don't think you'll enjoy being here, so if you want to leave, be my guest."

At this, Sonja rises abruptly from her seat and marches toward the closed door, as if to leave. At the last moment, she stops and turns back to face Chief Wayne defiantly.

"OK, OK," she concedes irritably. "You know I can't go anywhere else. Your department is the only one which would take me, because of my discipline problems."

"I know," Chief Wayne nods. "And you should

know I didn't want you here. The city council is behind your presence here, and little lady, all I want is a good reason to ship you back to Washington."

"Then I'll save you the trouble," Sonja counters, reaching again for the door handle.

"Go ahead, run back to the woodpile," Chief Wayne taunts knowing that she would change her direction with his little push.

Sonja froze, rage flashes across her features. "What did you say?" she demands through gritted teeth.

"Go ahead, run back to the woodpile," the Chief repeats slowly knowing she needs that provocation to motivate her in the right direction.

"That's what I thought you said." Sonja's voice shakes with anger. "I may be from Washington, but I know a racist remark when I hear it."

Chief Wayne holds up his hands innocently.

"Racist, little lady, 'round these parts I'm a card carrying member of the ACLU." He smirks before adding, "Now, do you want the job or not?"

Sonja hesitates, and then replies sternly, "Yes, I want the job."

"Alright then." Chief Wayne gestures to a massive book on the shelf. "You see that book over there?"

Sonja walks over and retrieved the heavy volume.

"This one?" she asks.

"No, that one," Wayne corrects, pointing instead to an even larger tome.

"That's the laws and rules of this community. I expect you to know every one of them," he says.

"You're kidding, right?" Sonja scoffs in disbelief.

"Do I look like I would kid?" Chief Wayne replies gruffly, standing up from his desk. "Now, it's time for you to go from the frying pan into the fire. Let's go meet your new partners."

Chief Wayne marches out of his office; Sonja follows behind clutching the giant book of laws to her chest.

"Everyone gather round," Chief Wayne announces to the squad room. "First, Jimmy, I want you to throw away the paperwork on that disturbing the peace charge. I'm letting her go."

Jimmy nods, moving quickly to comply.

"Next," Chief Wayne continues. "Bear, Jimmy, Jesse, and all of you, meet the newest member of the Henton Police Department – Officer Sonja Hemings."

Looks of disbelief form almost like a chain of dominoes falling across the faces of Jimmy, Jesse, Bear and all the men present. You could see the thoughts in their eyes: A woman police officer, an African-American police officer, a liberal, a hippy, a feminist, and a foreigner …

Sun Motel

Chapter Nine

Chief Wayne's patrol car rumbles up the gravel driveway of the Sun Motel at the edge of town. The aging two-story motel has seen better days, with peeling paint and overgrown weeds encroaching on the parking lot.

Chief Wayne cuts the engine and steps out into the oppressive heat, leaning against his car door. Across the lot, the motel room door swings open and Mr. James Harris emerges, briefcase in hand. Harris' polished dress shoes looked out of place sinking into the loose gravel as he made his way to the waiting patrol car. His posture was rigid, his clean-shaven jaw clenched.

Chief Wayne doesn't even wait for his arrival at the car. He seats himself back in the driver seat, rolls down the passenger window and asks through the open window. "Are you ready Mr. Harris?"

"Yes Chief, let's go," Harris replies curtly, his impatience evident. His large frame folded into the passenger seat, knees pressed against the dash.

Chief Wayne offers no small talk as the car crunches back down the drive in a cloud of dust.

A short time later, they pull onto a long dirt driveway leading to a weathered farmhouse and barn. In the front yard, a middle-aged black man looked up from the Farmall tractor engine he was repairing, wiping the grease from his strong hands. His faded denim overalls had seen years of hard work in the fields.

Chief Wayne stepped out and calls warmly, "Howard, how are you?"

"Fine, Chief. What are you doing out this way?" Howard Moses replies.

Though his tone was friendly, his eyes betray wariness at this unexpected visit.

"Well, this is James Harris and he wants to speak to you about buying your place," Chief Wayne explains plainly.

Moses glances between the two men, hesitant. But his years had taught him to mask any apprehension. He extends a dirt-smudged hand to Harris.

"Mr. Harris," he says evenly.

Harris gives a brief, limp handshake. "A pleasure," he says in a tone that suggests otherwise.

After a few minutes of talk seated on the front porch, it seems a deal is struck. Their business concludes for now, Chief Wayne and Harris retreat to the car.

A short while later, they pull up in front of a tidy, white farmhouse, its lawn neatly mowed. They get out and knock on the door. It wasn't long before another land deal was in the works. As they turn around, the older white man they had been talking with ambles out towards the mailbox. Though older, the short thin-framed man in blue coveralls, looked stout and muscular for his age.

"Mr. Sherrill, I know we won't have any problem getting the papers signed by tomorrow," Harris calls through the open window, an assurance and expectation.

"I sure appreciate you coming by. This is really an answer to prayer," Mr. Sherrill replies gratefully with a broad smile.

"See you, Mr. Sherrill," Chief Wayne adds warmly as they pull away.

"Thanks Chief! We'll be talking with you, Mr. Harris," Sherrill yelled after them, visibly relieved.

As the patrol car heads toward the Confederate Highway, an uncomfortable silence hangs between Wayne and Harris. The Chief keeps his eyes fixed on the road, trying not to imagine what dealings were happening behind the scenes.

He clenches the wheel tighter; his knuckles whiten as the near closer and closer to Ithaca. Wayne feels like a pawn abetting a larger play beyond his control. But this was Harris's town now – and Wayne just had to go along for the ride.

The imposing Ithaca archway it's wrought iron gates come into view as Chief Wayne's patrol car rumbles up the tree-lined drive. Gravel crackles under the tires, announcing their arrival at the stately white-columned mansion that had stood for

Ithaca Gate

over a century.

Jesse Wilson's sedan is parked in front, glinting in the shade of the massive oaks. Chief Wayne cuts the engine and steps out into the humid air, heavy with the scent of magnolias.

Harris extricates his tall frame from the passenger seat, straightening his suit jacket with a jerk.

Inside the home's pristine kitchen, delicate china clinks as Miss Allie arranges plates of sugar and chocolate chip cookies on a silver platter. The cookies' sweet aroma mingles with the faint traces of a peck of squeezed lemons used to create a large pitcher of lemonade. Miss Allie pauses to inspect the tea tray; wisps of silver-white hair framing her finely lined face.

"It's ready, Craven," she calls softly to the dutiful butler waiting nearby. Craven nods and pushes the teacart out ahead of her towards the parlor room where Jesse waits.

Jesse rises respectfully as Miss Allie enters the floral-papered room. "Would you like a fresh-baked chocolate chip cookie?" she offers with a gracious smile, extending the platter. "I know they are your favorite."

"Thank you," Jesse replies, selecting a couple of the treats and pouring himself a glass of lemonade. Craven silently glides out and closes the door, leaving aunt and nephew to converse privately.

"You know son, I'm not going to sell," Miss Allie states resolutely. "I'll meet with the man out of courtesy, but my mind is made up."

Before Jesse could reply, a knock came at the door that echoes down the wood-paneled hallway.

"Craven," Miss Allie calls, realizing their appointment had arrived.

"I've got it ma'am," Craven's muffled voice responds promptly. A moment later, the sitting room door opens to reveal Chief Wayne, followed by Mr. Harris and Craven.

"Miss Allie," Chief Wayne greets with familiar warmth.

"This is Mr. Harris. I believe you've met," he continues, with an edge of discomfort.

"How do you do?" Harris inquires politely, though his eyes held cold calculation. Miss Allie offers only a cursory nod in response.

"This is Miss Allie's nephew, Officer Jesse Wilson," Chief Wayne adds, gesturing.

"Yes, we've met also," Harris, acknowledges briskly.

"I hope there's no hard feelings," he offers to Jesse insincerely, extending a hand.

Jesse eyes him coldly, ignoring the gesture until a prompt from Chief Wayne forces a brisk handshake.

Miss Allie settled into the high-backed armchair, her fingers resting lightly on the armrests as she regarded Harris with measured calm.

Craven stood just behind her, his expression unreadable as he lifted the tray and offered a glass to each guest in succession.

Harris took a careful sip, savoring the taste before setting his glass on the mahogany side table and turns his attention back to Miss Allie.

"Miss Wilson," Harris began smoothly, folding his hands, "Ithaca is a remarkable estate, but I can't help but notice the signs of age upon it. I represent a company interested in purchasing your house and land. We are prepared to make a very substantial offer."

"Mr. Harris, I'm sure your offer is fair, but I'm not interested in selling," Miss Allie replies evenly, her genteel manner belying the steel in her tone; she picks up her glass and takes a long slow drink.

Miss Allie's sharp blue eyes didn't waver as she says, "Mr. Harris, Ithaca has stood for generations, and it will continue to stand long after I am gone."

Harris chuckled lightly, leaning forward with a knowing smile. "I admire your dedication, Miss Wilson, but surely you see that maintaining an estate of this size is a burden."

Craven shifted slightly, his deep brown eyes narrowing as he listened in silence.

"At least let me show you the figures," Harris insists with forced charm.

"Thank you, no!" Miss Allie responds emphatically. "I am not selling." She moves decisively towards the door. "Good day, gentlemen. Craven will show you out."

With that, she exits, leaving the men standing awkwardly. Harris fumes silently at this dismissal while the Chief finds sudden interest in the floral wallpaper. He then with great ease finishes his glass of lemonade, as Harris stands flabbergasted. The Chief eases over to the teacart and slips a couple of more cookies in a napkin and places them in his pocket.

"Well Jesse, I will see you at the station later," he says. "Mr. Harris, we should be going."

As they walk towards the door, Jesse went up the

stairs to check on his aunt. Chief Wayne says, "Craven, I seem to remember we have an outstanding fishing engagement."

"Why yes, yes we do," he says. "We'll do it soon."

He closes the door behind them.

Some time later, a knock at the kitchen door interrupted Miss Allie's baking. She opened it to find two familiar but unexpected faces.

"Mr. Sherrill, Mr. Moses, how are you?" she exclaims warmly. "Why, it's been years since either of you paid a call."

The farmers remove their worn hats as they enter the cheerful kitchen. "Miss Allie, may we come in?" Sherrill asks solemnly.

"Why, of course," Allie replies, though her smile faded slightly seeing their dour expressions. She motions for them to sit at the well-worn table while she prepared tea.

"Miss Allie, we need to talk to you," Sherrill began heavily after they had settled. "It's about the land deal. We understand you're not going to sell." Miss Allie stills, realization dawning. She turns to face them. "That's right," she confirms simply.

Moses leans forward, his weathered hands clasped beseechingly. "You know the last few years have been bad for farmers. This is a chance for us to get out from under."

"Now boys, I know it's been hard, but money won't solve the problem. What about your families? Don't you want them to have strong roots?" Miss Allie implores earnestly.

Sherrill's face darkens with resentment. "It's not roots we need, it's food and clothes. We're not like you with a big mansion and chests of gold lying around."

Miss Allie drew herself up, affronted. "Mr. Sherrill!"

"I believe it's time for you to leave," she states firmly, opening the door. The men stand slowly; shame mixes with defiance on their faces. "It's not over, Miss Allie. Not by a long shot," Sherrill warns ominously as they exit.

Miss Allie meets his stare. "Yes, gentlemen, it is," she replies with finality, closing the door firmly between them.

"Ithaca's Legacy"

Henton Police Department

Chapter Ten

Chief Wayne sat in his worn, green, leather-upholstered chair in the Henton Police Department office, reviewing files, when a knock sounds at the open door. He glances up to see Commissioner George Hargrove's round, sweat-beaded face peers into the office.

"Chief, you got a minute?" Hargrove asks brusquely.

"Sure, George. Come in," Wayne beckons, though his jaw tightens instinctively.

Hargrove enters and perches on the edge of the visitor's chair. "I understand Miss Wilson didn't want to sell," he says, cutting right to the point.

Wayne leans back, steepling his fingers. "Yeah, Miss Allie's proud of her home, and you know she should be – it's one of the oldest places around here."

Hargrove nods impatiently. "Well, Chief, I came hoping you might persuade Jesse to talk to his aunt about selling."

Wayne's eyes narrow, "George, I believe such a request may endanger my regard for your high office," he replies evenly. "I do appreciate you coming by though – and be sure to wish Mr. Harris luck finding a new location."

His meaning clear, Wayne holds Hargrove's gaze

steadily until the Commissioner rises and departs without another word.

Not long after, Jesse appears in the doorway, looking conflicted. "Chief, do you think I'm doing the right thing leaving the decision about the land deal to Aunt Allie?" he asks.

Wayne considers him thoughtfully. "Jesse, do you remember when you were a teenager and needed someone to talk to? Whom did you go to?" "Either Aunt Allie or Craven," Jesse replies.

"You trusted them then, didn't you?" Wayne asks.

Jesse nods. "Yes Chief, nothing's different now – thanks," he says appreciatively, seeming relieved by the wisdom.

Ithaca Gate

Later at Ithaca, soft lamplight illuminates Miss Allie's face as she sits brushing her long silver-white hair before bed. A knock sounds at her bedroom door. "Yes?" she calls.

Craven entered with his usual decorum and asks. "Would you like anything before you rest, Miss Allie?"

"No thank you, Craven," She hesitates before adding, "Craven, are you glad about my decision?"

"Yes ma'am, I sure am," he affirms. "I'm going to lock up the garden shed before I turn in. Good night."

"Good night," Miss Allie replies as he exits.

Moments later under the moon's dim glow, Craven's silhouette approaches the small tool shed at the edge of Ithaca's manicured gardens. As he steps closer to the shed, he thinks he hears a man's voice. "Is anyone there," he calls. He looks around the area and nothing seems out of place, so he just assumes, he imagined the voice. As his hand grasps the doorknob, the night explodes into a massive fire-ball, the shed bursting into flames that lights up the darkness.

"Ithaca's Legacy"

Ithaca Garden Shed

Chapter Eleven

The last dying embers snap and crackle as the volunteer firemen work to extinguish the flames engulfing the old wooden garden shed at the edge of Ithaca's garden. Light plumes of gray smoke billow up into the night sky, carrying the heavy stench of kerosene.

Miss Allie stood nearby; her face ashen with shock, as Bear wraps a comforting arm around her shoulders. She couldn't tear her eyes away from the scene before her – Craven's limp body being loaded into the back of the ambulance. The sound of the doors slamming jolts her from her stupor.

Chief Wayne, with his brow creased with worry, approaches Miss Allie as the ambulance pulls away into the night. "What happened? Are you alright?" His voice was gentle but firm, the voice of someone accustomed to taking charge in a crisis.

Before Miss Allie could respond, Bear spoke up in his signature-rumbling baritone, "She's not hurt, Chief. It was Craven."

At that moment, the crunch of tires on gravel announces the arrival of Jesse's car. He jumps out, still dressed in civilian clothes, and ran over to Miss Allie. His handsome face is twisted with concern as he takes her in his arms. "Aunt Allie, are you okay? What happened here?"

Miss Allie finally lets the tears flow. Her slight frame shakes with sobs as she clings to her nephew. Over her shoulder, Jesse exchanges a grim look with Bear and Chief Wayne. They all know something sinister had happened here tonight. And they are determined to get to the bottom of it.

Miss Allie's sobs eventually subside into shaky breaths as Jesse holds her. Chief Wayne places a reassuring hand on her shoulder as he says, "Don't you worry Miss Allie, we'll get to the bottom of this. I promise you that."

His voice is filled with kindness and determination. Miss Allie manages a small nod, dabbing at her eyes with a handkerchief.

Just then, Officers Jimmy and Sonja approach the Chief. "Chief, we didn't find much of anything around the shed," Jimmy reports.

Sonja adds, "You'll likely know more once the arson investigators go over the site."

Wayne frowns, the deep wrinkles in his weathered face becoming more pronounced. "Officer Hemings, we are the arson investigators. This is Henton, not Atlanta."

Chagrined, Sonja replies, "Of course, Chief. What about a chemical analysis then?"

Wayne turns to Bear with a knowing look. "Bear, what do you think? What chemical was involved here?"

Bear lifts his large nose into the air and took a few sniffs. "Kerosene," he pronounces in his baritone voice.

"Now why don't you two go take another look around, see if you can find any evidence of kerosene," instructs Chief Wayne.

"Yes Chief," Jimmy says. The two officers head off into the darkness.

Chief Wayne turns back to Bear. "Craven said something about two men before he passed out. Check the area for any tracks or clues."

Bear hesitates. "But Chief, with all the firemen around..."

"I know," Wayne sighs, "but take a look anyway."

Chief Wayne joins Miss Allie and Jesse, who are huddled together comforting each other.

"How could this happen?" Miss Allie cries, her voice quivering. "Who would want to hurt Craven?"

"I don't know Miss Allie, but we're going to find out, no matter what it takes," Chief Wayne says gently. Though he spoke calmly, his jaw is tight with suppressed anger at what was done to his friend.

Jesse steps in, "Why don't I take you inside where it's warm, Aunt Allie? You need to get some rest after the shock you've had."

Chief Wayne nods approvingly. "That's a fine idea. You both could use some sleep instead of standing out here in the cold night air."

But Miss Allie protests, "I couldn't possibly sleep! I need to get to the hospital right away. But who will drive me?"

"I'll take you there myself, don't you worry," Jesse reassures her.

Miss Allie finally relents with a weary sigh. Jesse guides her towards his car, keeping a supportive arm around her slender shoulders.

Later, at the hospital, Miss Allie stares vacantly out the window of the waiting room. She is pale and shaken, trying to make sense of the night's horrific events.

Jesse and Chief Wayne speak in hushed tones with Dr. Dodd, the town's energetic family doctor who also serves as county coroner. After conferring with them, Dr. Dodd approaches Miss Allie.

"Miss Allie, please have a seat. You need to rest," he urges gently. When she reluctantly sat, he continues, "Craven is unconscious but stable. He's very lucky – the blow he took could have easily killed him."

"May I see him?" Miss Allie pleads, fresh tears shining in her eyes.

"Yes, just for a minute," Dr. Dodd consents.

Chief Wayne turns to Dr. Dodd, his brow furrows. "Doctor, could you tell anything about Craven's assailant from the blow he received?"

Dr. Dodd considers for a moment before responding. "Only that whoever struck him was either not very strong or tall. That blow could have easily been fatal had it been delivered with more force."

Jesse leaves the doctor's side and goes to check on Miss Allie in Craven's room.

In the dim hospital room, Craven lays unconscious in the bed. His head is wrapped in white bandages, though his forehead remained exposed. Miss Allie stands over him, her expression sorrowful. Gently, she bends down and presses a soft kiss to his forehead.

At that moment, Jesse quietly enters the room. Seeing his aunt's tender gesture, he pauses just inside the doorway, not wanting to intrude, and also not wanting her to know he saw it.

Once Miss Allie stood upright again, Jesse steps forward. "Aunt Allie, it's time to go," he says softly.

Miss Allie turns to face him as Jesse comes to stand by her side. His handsome face is kind and full of concern.

"Son, you know Craven and I have always been so close, like brother and sister," Miss Allie begins, sitting down in the chair beside the bed. Jesse sits down next to her and listens intently as she continues.

"His great-grandfather died right alongside mine

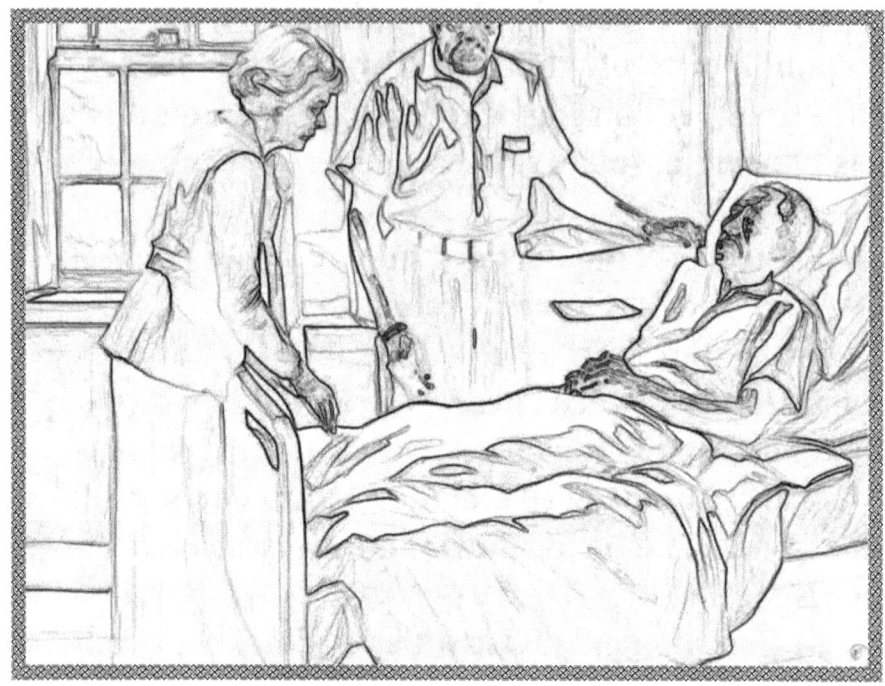

Craven's Hospital Room

at Ithaca. We grew up together in a way. He and
your grandfather were inseparable as boys." She
gave a wistful smile at the memories.

"Craven and I, well, we were always a little out
of place back then. When we were young we were
ahead of our times, yet now we seem behind the
times in our old age," she says as her smile fades
and a tear rolls down her cheek. "I just don't know
what I'd do if I lost him."

At that, Miss Allie breaks down sobbing. Jesse
immediately stands and grasps her shoulders com-
fortingly from behind. Together they keep a silent

vigil over Craven's still form, watching the barely perceptible rise and fall of his chest.

"Ithaca's Legacy"

Henton Police Department

Chapter Twelve

Chief Wayne sits at his desk in the Henton Police Station, his brow furrowed in concentration as he reviews notes on the previous night's disturbing events. The heavy oaken door creaks open and Bear lumbers in; his mountainous frame nearly fills the doorway.

"I just don't know what could have been the motive for the arson and assault. Nothing was stolen. I been over that site again and again," he rumbles in his deep baritone.

Wayne leans back in his chair, the old springs squeak in protest. "Were you able to find any finger-prints on that board that had Craven's blood on it?" he inquires.

"There were some smudges, but no distinct prints," Bear replies with a shake of his head.

Just then, the door bursts open again, banging against the wall. Jesse charges in, face flush with excitement.

"Chief, Aunt Allie told me that Mr. Sherrill and Mr. Moses were by to see her yesterday afternoon, and – Mr. Sherrill made a threatening remark as he left," he says.

Bear turns to Wayne with a knowing look and says, "Those are the two who wanted Miss Allie's to sell her land."

Wayne nods grimly, deep creases lining his weathered face as he says, "Yeah, and both wanted to sell."

"And Aunt Allie didn't," Jesse adds pointedly.

Pushing back his chair, Chief Wayne stands.

"Jesse, have Ellison run out and let both of them know, I want to see them both this afternoon at three," he says.

After Jesse hurries out, Wayne exchanges a determined look with Bear.

"It's time to turn up the heat on the suspects," he says.

Miss Allie makes her way down the grand staircase into the front hall. The chime of the doorbell echoes through the empty house. When she arrives, she finds the mail had been dropped through the slot. Sifting through it she finds bills, and sales circulars until one envelope caught her eye. Her face fell as she reads the bold red letters spelling out "Foreclosure Notice."

With a heavy heart, Miss Allie drifts across the receiving hall, and sits down in a solitary chair backed up to the staircase facing the painting of her father and those before him. She had put on a gallant front for everyone for some time. Except for the common areas where guests might wonder – the parlor, the library and the kitchen, receiving hall, her bedroom, and the car, she was empting the

Ithaca Front Hall

house of the priceless antiques, jewelry, and artwork for some time to meet the rising expenses. She had even quietly traveled out of town and took a mortgage on Ithaca away from prying eyes and wagging tongues to try to keep things going. She even keeps the situation from Jesse. Craven is the only one who is aware of her selling things off but even he did not know about the mortgage. He kept the clandestine sales quiet not sharing with the other village residents. As they cleared out a room, Miss Allie would lock the door and Craven would tell the maids not to bother with that room anymore. Her eyes settle on the distinguished portrait of her great grandfather.

"If only you knew how hard it's been to hold onto your land and this house," she confides to the painting. "Dad's money ran out. There is no income nowadays, just outgo. I've sold almost every piece of furniture, every last heirloom. And now I've nearly lost Craven too." She gazes up at the wise eyes of her ancestor. "What should I do, Granddad?"

Later that afternoon, Chief Wayne, Jesse, and Officer Jimmy question Mr. Moses in the office with the door closed. Sherrill impatiently waits his turn in the hallway, nervously wringing his hands.

Wayne's weathered face is stern as he asked, "Mr. Moses, were you at Miss Allie's yesterday?"

Moses shifts uneasily in his seat. "Yes sir, in the afternoon around one or two o'clock."

Jesse leans forward intently. "Are you sure it wasn't 9 or 10 last night?"

Chief Wayne silences Jesse with a sharp look before turning back to Moses.

"Were you at Miss Allie's last night?" Wayne asks.

Moses shifts nervously. "No, no I wasn't. I wouldn't have done anything to hurt Miss Allie or Craven."

"Did you threaten Miss Allie?"

"No, sir," Moses replies timidly.

Officer Jimmy leans forward and asks, "Did Mr. Sherrill?"

"I don't think he meant to," Sherrill says.

"So he did?" Wayne presses.

"Well, I-" Moses stumbles over his words.

"Howard," Wayne says sternly.

"Yes, he did," Moses finally admits.

Chief Wayne stood up. "Jesse, take Mr. Moses' statement then release him. Send Mr. Sherrill and Bear in."

After Jesse escorts Moses out, Bear enters with a defiant-looking Sherrill and sits him down.

"I don't understand why I'm here," Sherrill says testily to Chief Wayne.

"There was a fire and assault near your property last night. We just have some questions," Wayne replies evenly.

Sherrill visibly relaxes, thinking he was no longer a suspect.

Bear leans forward intently. "We know you visited Miss Allie yesterday around 2 p.m. What for?"

"Howard and I went to persuade her to sell her land, so we could sell ours," Sherrill explains.

"Did you need to sell badly enough to commit arson and assault?" Bear presses.

"I didn't do either!" Sherrill insists angrily.

Chief Wayne's expression is stone. "Didn't you threaten Miss Allie?"

Sherrill sputters, "Yes...no.. maybe."

"You don't know?" Wayne asks sharply.

Sherrill just turns away silently. Bear and Wayne exchange a look.

"All right Billy," Chief Wayne says. "You can collect your thoughts in one of our jail cells."

Bear escorts the protesting Sherrill out to stew downstairs.

Open Door Cafe

Chapter Thirteen

Chief Wayne enters the cozy Open Door Cafe, the bells on the door announces his arrival.

"Hi Chief, would you like some coffee?" asks Pearly Mae, who had owned the cafe for as long as anyone in town could remember. Her plump cheeks are rosy as she smiles and reaches for the glass pot behind the counter, ready to pour him a cup. Wayne approaches the counter.

"No thanks, I just stopped by to grab my hat. Left it here this morning," he says.

Pearly Mae nods knowingly. "Chief, Bob has been asking after you all afternoon," she says, gesturing with a tilt of her head towards the back of the restaurant where Bob sits alone at a table, nursing a cup of coffee with his back to the door.

Glancing over his shoulder, Wayne spots Bob sitting alone at a table in his Bibb overalls, sporting his favorite hat. "I believe I will take that cup of coffee after all," Wayne concedes, picking up a faded blue mug from the shelf behind the counter. The porcelain clattered softly as Pearly Mae dutifully fills it to the brim with the rich, earthy brew. Steam curls up in wispy tendrils, carrying the bitter aroma.

Coffee in hand, Wayne makes his way across the dining room. "Hello Bob," he greets him as he reaches the table. "Mind if I join you?"

Bob's face lit up at the sight of the police chief. His slate blue eyes crinkled at the corners as he grinned broadly. "Please do, Chief!"

Wayne settles into the chair opposite Bob. He took a tentative sip of the scalding coffee strong and black as pitch. It's just the way he likes it. He places the mug back down.

"How goes the investigation on Miss Allie's?" Bob asks eagerly, getting straight to the point, his leg jitters restlessly under the table. It was clear from his posture he had information to share.

"Pretty good," Wayne replies casually, keeping his cards close to his chest.

Bob struggles visibly to contain his excitement, like a hound straining against a leash trying to pick up a scent. "Chief, I have a huntin' buddy who was out in those woods by Miss Allie's the other night."

Wayne's interest is piqued, though his expression remains neutral. "The night of the fire?" he asks.

"Yeah," Bob nods, scratching the back of his neck. "He was a little concerned about saying anything 'cause what he was huntin' was a little out of season."

Wayne suppresses a wry smile. "Um-hmm," he intones knowingly, taking another sip of coffee.

"Well," Bob continues, clearly more at ease now, "he says he saw two men running through the woods away from Miss Allie's. He didn't see but one of them real clear, but he recognized him." Bob pauses for effect. "He says it was Cleo Lyons."

Wayne leans back in his chair, the wood creaking under his shifting weight as he pretends to search his memory. "Cleo Lyons," he repeats slowly. "That name sure sounds familiar."

"Don't you remember last year's Governor's rally?" Bob prods excitedly.

The details click into place in Wayne's mind. "Wasn't he the one who sawed the legs of the platform because he didn't like the candidate?" he asks.

Bob laughs heartily, his shoulders shake. "Yeah, and as soon as that feller got up there to speak the whole bottom fell out!"

Wayne allows a small smile. "I remember him now. Well, you tell your huntin' buddy thanks," he says, standing up from the table and laying a few bills next to his half-finished coffee. "Oh, and tell him not to be doing any more huntin' a little out of season."

"He won't, he won't," Bob promises earnestly to himself, still chuckling as Wayne tips the brim of his hat and heads out the door.

Chief Wayne steps briskly through the front door of the Henton Police Department, the heavy oak slab swings shut behind him with a thud that rattles the glass panes.

Jimmy Ellison is stationed at the front desk, fan-

Henton Police Squad Room

ning himself with a folded newspaper. He hastily composes himself when he sees the chief enter.

"Jimmy, look in the files and find the current address for a Cleo Lyons," Wayne instructs. "When you find it, go pick him up for questioning."

"Yes sir, I'll get right on it!" Jimmy confirms enthusiastically, tossing aside the newspaper, he hurries over to the tall filing cabinets along the back wall, eager to please the chief.

Wayne continues on through the squad room towards his office, the heels of his boots thud dully on the scuffed tile floors.

Later, Wayne sits at his desk scanning over a report when a knock sounds at his door. "Come in," he calls out.

The door swings open and Bear lumbers in. Wayne sets the papers aside and leans forward, steepling his fingers.

"Bear, I think we've got our other man," he announces without preamble.

Bear's bushy eyebrows shoot up in surprise as he asks, "Who?"

"I got a tip that Cleo Lyons was running away from Miss Allie's the night of the fire," Wayne explains. "I sent the boys out to get him."

Suddenly a commotion arises from the squad room outside. Muffled shouts and scuffling sounds filter through the closed office door. Bear and Wayne exchange a look before quickly getting to their feet and stepping out to investigate.

There they found Officers Sonja Hemings and Jimmy Ellison wrestling to restrain a disheveled man in cuffs, their uniforms are smeared with dirt from the tussle. Bear lunges forward to help subdue the struggling man.

"Alright, you settle down now," Bear rumbles, his beefy hands clamp down on the man's shoulders. The man instantly stills under Bear's vise-like grip.

Chief Wayne looks on with concern. "What's going on out here?"

"Mr. Lyons didn't want to come, sir," Sonja explained breathlessly, tucking the tail of her blue shirt back under her belt.

Jimmy flashes a sly grin, adjusting his askew sunglasses, as he shares, "We had to convince him, sir."

Bear gives a snort of laughter as he keeps a firm hold on the now docile suspect. "I'm not sure which of you look more convinced."

"Y'all get cleaned up," Wayne instructs Sonja and Jimmy. "Bear, bring him into my office."

Wayne leads the way back into his office. Bear forces Cleo Lyons down into the chair across from the chief's desk before taking up position standing behind him. His massive arms cross over his chest. Wayne perches on the edge of his desk and fixes Lyons with a piercing stare.

"Cleo, I understand you paid a late night visit to Miss Allie's the other night," Wayne says.

Lyons gawks, caught off guard by the accusation. "Who told you that?" he blurts out before he could stop himself.

"We have another man in custody," Wayne informs him cryptically.

Lyons shifts anxiously in his seat. "He's lying!" he insists hotly. "I was nowhere near Miss Allie's. I was out huntin' with some friends."

Amusement glints in Wayne's eyes, though his face remains impassive. "Funny you should say that. So was the man who told us about you."

Trapped, Lyons resorts to silence. "I had nothing

to do with the fire," he mutters sullenly. "And I don't have anymore to say 'til I speak to my lawyer."

Wayne sighs, accustomed to this familiar dance.

"That's fine," he says evenly. "I believe you and I have been at this point before. Bear, let Mr. Lyons call his lawyer, then take him down."

Wayne steps closer to Bear and lowers his voice to say, "Put him in a cell where he won't see the other suspect."

Bear nods saying "Yes sir." He clamps one of his massive paws down on Lyons' bony shoulder. "Come on," he rumbled, steering the defeated man out the door.

Sun Motel

Chapter Fourteen

The peeling paint and rusted sign for the Sun Motel flicker erratically in the gathering dusk as Commissioner George Hargrove approaches room 12. His polished leather shoes sink into the crusty carpet outside the door as he raises his hand to knock.

"It's open," calls a gruff voice from within.

Hargrove turns the tarnished brass knob and enters the dim, stuffy room. In the flickering light of the ancient TV, he made out the imposing silhouette of James Harris sprawled on the sagging bed.

"I've just been checking some records and found the old lady is delinquent on her taxes," Hargrove announces, removing his hat as he stands awkwardly just inside the door. "Twelve months ago, Sam Windom took over the tax lien. I understand that he is in the foreclosure process."

Harris sits up, suddenly interested. At just over six feet with a lean muscular build, he cuts an intimidating figure.

"That's great!" he exclaims, flashing a predatory grin. "When we get this project finished, we'll both make a fortune. I'll get over to his office first thing in the morning to make a deal."

Hargrove shifts his weight from one foot to the other, betraying his discomfort. "I'll meet with the

143

rest of the board to push through the building permits," he murmurs, staring down at his polished wingtips.

"Don't worry, we'll have that place bulldozed before they know what hit them," Harris declares confidently, laying back down and lacing his hands behind his head.

Hargrove nods mutely and slips back out into the night, leaving the door to bang closed behind him.

The waiting room of Henton Hospital smells strongly of bleach and stale air. Chief Wayne leans

Henton Hospital

against the mint green wall beneath a buzzing fluo-
rescent light, boots crossed at the ankle. His face is
creased with worry beneath his tan Stetson.

Beside him sits the diminutive figure of Miss
Allie, primly perched on the edge of a wooden chair.
Stray wisps of silver-white hair peek out from
beneath her flowered hat as she clutches her purse
tightly in her lap.

At the squeak of rubber-soled shoes on tile, they
both look up expectantly as Dr. Richard Dodd
enters. Wayne straightens, tugging at the hem of his
jacket.

"Craven's awake, but he's very weak," Dodd
reports, his normally jovial face uncharacteristically
grim. "You can have just a minute with him."

Wayne offers his arm to help Miss Allie rise.
Together with Jesse Wilson, they follow Dr. Dodd
down the sterile corridor to Craven's room.

Inside, the pale figure of Craven Wilson lay
motionless amidst the maze of tubes and wires. At
their entrance, Miss Allie immediately rushes to his
bedside. Gently clasping his limp hand in her own
gnarled fingers, she asks tremulously, "Where have
you been for so long?"

Craven's eyes flutter open, glassy and unfocused.
"I've been home," he murmurs weakly.
"Home...years ago."

Jesse moves closer, broad shoulders hunched

beneath his uniform. "Crav, we need to ask you some questions about the men who did this," he says gently.

Craven gives a faint nod. "I didn't see them," he whispers. "But I heard one of them. His voice...it sticks in my head like the pain I feel."

"Do you remember what he said?" Jesse presses. Beside him, Wayne leans in intently.

Craven's eyes drift closed as he struggles to remember.

"I was thrown by the explosion," he says. "When I came to myself, that's when I heard them. It was something like, 'That old lady will be no problem after this.' I pushed myself to my feet and that's when I was hit from behind."

A spasm of pain creases his pale features as he continues, "Then I went out until I walked towards y'all."

Wayne nods, placing a weathered hand on Craven's shoulder. "Thank you. You get some rest now." He exchanged a knowing look with Jesse, and then quietly left the room.

Jesse turns to Miss Allie. "We better go and let Crav rest awhile," he says gently.

Miss Allie clasps Craven's limp hand to her cheek. "May I stay?" she pleads; unshed tears glistening in her eyes. "I'll sit quietly – I want to stay."

Southern Crossing

Jesse hesitates. "I'll ask the doctor," he acquiesces. With a final pat on Craven's shoulder, he too departs.

"Ithaca's Legacy"

Henton Police Department

Chapter Fifteen

Back at the station later that afternoon, Jimmy and Sonja are stationed at the front counter when an unfamiliar man strides through the doors, enveloped in a cloud of expensive cologne.

"Yes sir, what can I do for you?" Jimmy asks with forced politeness, discreetly nudging a powdered doughnut out of sight beneath some papers.

"Is Chief Wayne in?" the man demands brusquely.

"Yes sir, just a moment." Jimmy sends Sonja scurrying to fetch the chief.

She returns shortly with Chief Wayne in tow, his salt-and-pepper hair neatly combed. Sonja quietly resumes her duties as Wayne approaches the counter, greeting the man, "Mr. Harris, how goes the developing?"

Harris flashes a predatory smile, shark-like within the frame of his chiseled features. "Real well! I just dropped by to let you know we're going to break ground in the morning," he says.

Surprise flickers across Wayne's normally stoic face. "You are? Where?"

"At Ithaca," Harris replies smugly, clearly relishing the reaction.

Wayne's thick eyebrows draw together in a frown as he reacts, "But Miss Allie wasn't going to sell."

"I bought her tax lien and I foreclose on Friday at noon," Harris informs him matter-of-factly, checking his expensive watch. "If she doesn't pay by then, we break ground at 12:01. I hope you can be there."

With a curt parting nod, Harris strides back out of the station, expensive leather shoes squeaking on the scuffed floors.

Jaw clenches Wayne turns to Sonja. "Get Jesse on the phone, he's at the hospital."

Sonja swiftly moves to comply as Wayne retreats grimly to his office; the door slams heavily behind him.

In the sterile stillness of Craven's hospital room, Miss Allie keeps her frail, veined hand wrapped gently around his. Her feather-soft silver-white curls peek out from beneath her flowered hat as she maintains her bedside vigil.

The door creaks open and Jesse Wilson enters quietly. His handsome features have a seriousness about them that belies his years. It is the look of someone forced to grow up too fast.

"Aunt Allie, the Chief just called," Jesse says grimly, hat in hand. "He says Mr. Harris bought your tax lien. If you don't pay by Friday he's taking the property."

Hearing this, Craven stirs; his once powerful

Henton Hospital

frame now diminished against the stark white sheets. "They're taking our home?" he asks, his voice ragged with emotion.

"Not if I can stop them," Jesse vows, his jaw set with determination. Miss Allie reaches out and grasps Jesse's arm. Her genteel manner commands attention. "You can't, son," she says resignedly. "The bill is fifty thousand dollars."

Jesse gasps, clearly stunned by the figure.

"How did it get that big?" he asks.

"Well, the old tax commissioner, Mr. Newton,

agreed to let me pay as I could several years ago," Miss Allie explains. "If we just had a small house and a few acres of land, it wouldn't be so much, but we have our manor house, our village and so many acres. I pay on every square foot, every acre, every building whether in use or not. The bill just got a little out of hand. So, he helped me find a man named Sam Windom down in Biloxi that bought the lien and has been very kind through the years to allow me just to pay when I could."

Jesse runs a frustrated hand through his dark hair as he questions, "Why didn't you come to me?"

Miss Allie pats his hand soothingly. "I know you work hard and the money you make wouldn't have made a dent in the bill. I didn't want to worry you."

Jesse's shoulders slump in defeat. "I'll try to figure out something," he says half-heartedly before taking his leave.

Later at the Henton Savings Bank, Jesse sits tense as a coil in the loan officer's dreary office. The clock ticks loudly in the silence as he awaits the verdict. Finally the officer returns, smoothing his tie.

"Mr. Wilson, I'm sorry but you don't have enough equity in any of your property for us to make a secured loan," he states matter-of-factly.

Jesse surges to his feet in frustration. "Nothing?" he demands. "You mean after all the years I've been doing business with this bank, I can't get anything?"

Henton Savings Bank

The loan officer holds up his hands helplessly. "If I could help I would. Maybe a co-signer..." he offers lamely.

Jesse laughs bitterly and storms from the office.

Jesse's boots echo hollowly on the floors of the courthouse hallway as he approaches the heavy oaken door bearing the plaque "Horace Rigson – Tax Commissioner".

He hesitates, steeling himself, before grasping the brass knob and stepping inside. The office was dim and cluttered, smelling of dusty paper and worn leather. Behind an enormous desk piled high with precariously tilting stacks of files and paper sits

Henton Courthouse

Horace Rigson. Though only in his thirties, his rumpled suit, thinning hair, and hunched posture made
him seem older. He glances up in surprise as Jesse
enters.

"Mr. Rigson, may I talk to you a moment?" Jesse
asks without preamble, removes his hat and turns it
nervously in his hands.

"I bet it's about Aunt Allie's bill," Rigson says
knowingly, leaning back in his creaking leather
chair.

Jesse nods. "Yes. I was wondering if there was
some way that I could pay her bill on time." His
voice strains with tightly restrained emotion.

Rigson's eyes soften with sympathy, but he slowly
shakes his head. "I'm sorry, Jesse. There's nothing I
can do since Mr. Windom owns the lien and he sold
it to Mr. Harris. Only a full payment can stop the
process now."

Henton Police Department

Jesse's shoulders slump in defeat. "Thank you for your time," he murmurs tonelessly before replacing his hat and exiting the office. The heavy door falls shut with a note of grim finality.

Back at the station, Officers "Bear" Bryson and Jimmy Ellison look up with concern as a despondent Jesse enters the squad room.

"Jesse, how are you?" Jimmy ventures tentatively. His round, boyish face creases with worry.

Bear's craggy features mirror Jimmy's apprehension. "Is there anything we can do?" he rumbles in his gravelly baritone.

Lost in his own gloomy thoughts, Jesse didn't

seem to register their questions. Seeing his friend's distress, Jimmy gently guides him towards the evidence room, away from prying eyes.

Once inside the cramped, windowless space, Jimmy turns to Jesse. "Was there something you wanted to show me?" Jesse asks distractedly, glancing around at the rows of boxes and shelves.

Jimmy shakes his head. "No, Jesse. I just wanted to tell you, I spoke to Alicia and we have five thousand dollars put back we'd like you to have."

Jesse stares for a moment before collecting himself.

"That's awfully kind, but I couldn't take it," he demurs.

"If you need it it's yours," Jimmy insists earnestly.

Jesse places a grateful hand on his friend's shoulder. "Thank you, but I don't have a fifth of what the bill is."

Jimmy nods in understanding. "Well, if you need it..."

Leaving the offer hanging, Jimmy exits the evidence room. Alone, Jesse lingers a moment, warmed by his friend's generosity even as icy fingers of despair squeezed his heart.

The next morning at the hospital found a determined Craven attempting to dress himself despite Dr. Dodd's protests.

Henton Hospital

"Now Crav, you're not ready to be out of bed," Dodd cautions, trying to steer the weak but stubborn man back towards the mattress.

Craven shrugs off his hands. "Now look, Doc. I'm going, so either help me, or the nurses will have a heck of a time getting you out of this bed," he declares, a hint of his old spark returning.

Dodd laughs and holds up his hands in defeat. "Okay, let's get you ready and I'll take you to Ithaca myself," he says.

Inside the stately manor, Jesse descends the

"Ithaca's Legacy"

Ithaca Staircase

central staircase, polished wood smooth beneath his fingertips from decades of use. He had grown up within these walls under the doting care of his elderly Aunt Allie.

Reaching the foyer, he is greeted by Chief Wayne,

Allie prepares in her bedroom.

158

whose imposing frame dominates the ornate entry-way.

"Jesse," Wayne rumbles in his gravelly baritone. "Time to go." His craggy features are unreadable beneath the brim of his hat.

Jesse gives a terse nod, "Coming Chief" and turns to rouse Aunt Allie from her upstairs sitting room. The elegant old woman takes Wayne's offered arm, casting a longing look over her shoulder at the home she is being forced to abandon.

Out front, the crowd's murmurs swell as Aunt

Ithaca Manor House

Allie slowly emerges, escorted by Chief Wayne while Jesse brings up the rear. They ease her fragile frame into the waiting Ghost. As the vehicle crawls down the drive towards the arch, the heckling voices grew louder. The car pulls to a stop with Jesse getting out of the driver's seat. The Chief opens the back door, gets out and offers his hand to Miss Allie as she exits. They gather in front of the gate, a few feet from the heavy equipment that Harris has standing by.

Bear and Jimmy stand ready to intervene as the impatient Harris checks his watch again. Though not time, the driver possibly on Harris's cue, allows the bulldozer to lurch forward, striking the archway with a crack like thunder, sending up a cloud of dust and debris.

Ithaca Hidden Cellar

In the chaos, Aunt Allie cries out and rushes towards the crumbling stones. Jesse lunges after her but trips, plunging into a dark cavity revealed beneath the rubble. "Jesse!" she exclaims.

Wayne shouts, dropping to peer into the hole. "Can you hear me?"

"Yes sir, I'm fine!" Jesse's muffled voice echoes up. "Bring down a light!"

In moments, Chief Wayne, flashlight in hand, descends into the dark hole revealing to him the smell of a musty cellar and ancient stone stairs visible at his feet. Ancient dust swirls in the beam of light, revealing a small chamber filled with dozens of wooden crates. Prying one open, Wayne draws a sharp breath – it is filled to bursting with glinting gold coins.

"You'll never believe what we found," Jesse yells. "The legend's true."

"Praise the Lord!" Aunt Allie exclaims jubilantly from above, "Mr. Tax Commissioner, hurry, let's go down."

Horace with Miss Allie on his arm then come scrambling down the dark stairs at her urging. Rigson's eyes widen at the sight of the fortune before him. Craven and the doctor carefully lean over the hole peering down.

As they near some of the now opened crates, "Do you think this will cover the taxes?" Aunt Allie presses eagerly.

Rigson hesitates. "It will, but I'm afraid it doesn't belong to you, Miss Allie."

Chief Wayne intervened, "What are you saying, Horace?"

"Since it's Confederate Army gold, it's the property of the federal government now."

Jesse speaks up quickly, "When I was in school, we studied about there being a reward for finding the gold – 10 percent of what was found. And Aunt Allie, didn't the family story say that the Captain hid the family gold and silver with it too?"

"Yes, that's true," Allie says.

Rigson brightens as he adds, "You're right, Jesse, I'd forgot about that!"

"Jesse, sometime you surprise me," Wayne says with a smile.

"The finder's fee should easily cover the taxes and leave quite a bit considering how many crates are here and maybe the ledgers on the desk will tell us what's theirs and what's yours," Rigson says.

Allie stands at the open crate filled with gold coins.

"Jesse come here, hold out your hands." Allie reached into the crate and counts out 26 gold coins. "These should cover what is owed. I am giving them to you – Mr. Rigson in payment of the lien for Mr. Harris. We can settle the specifics later. What's the time?"

"11:59," says Mr. Rigson.

Footsteps echo from above. Harris' impatient voice rang out demanding to know what was happening, "What's going on? I've got a house to demolish."

"Maybe you do, but it's not here," Miss Allie yells back.

Commissioner Hargrove looks at Harris and yells to the Chief, "What's she talking about?"

Before anyone could respond, Craven cries out "Chief, Jesse, that's the voice!"

Realizing what he's recognized, Hargrove eases quickly towards his car.

The Chief yells up the stairs, "Arrest Mr. Hargrove."

In a blur, Bear detains the suspect, saying, "What's your hurry?" along with a protesting Harris.

The Chief made his way into the light of day followed by Rigson.

"Bear, take this Mr. Hargrove and Mr. Harris down to the station. I believe they can shed some light on our case," the Chief says.

He turns to the remaining crowd and yells, "Go on home now. Nothing else to see, no sale, no demolition and whatever else happens you can read about in next week's Henton Gazette. Now geeeet!"

"Ithaca's Legacy"

The Chief brings Craven down the stairs joining Aunt Allie and Jesse. Jesse found the old candles and oil lamps and had them burning. Amidst the flickering glow of flashlights, candles, and an oil lamp, countless crates of glittering treasure shine.

"What will you do with what's left, Miss Allie?" Wayne asks.

Allie seems to not hear his question; instead she looks at Jesse, pats his hand leaning on the counting desk and smiles. "It's time you and that boy of yours move back here. Jake needs to grow up here. And I want to see him do just that."

"What will you do with what's left, Miss Allie?" Wayne asks again.

"I believe Craven and I will make Ithaca what our Granddads wanted it to be," she says as she reached out and touched his shoulder.

She turns to an old photograph sitting atop the nearby counting desk, which had been idle since 1863 when her great grandfather last sat doing his sums.

Jesse looks to her quizzically. "What's did they want it to be, Aunt Allie?"

"A home, son, a home," she says.

Buy Other Books by
Randall Franks

A Mountain Pearl : Appalachian Reminiscing and Recipes
Whittlin' and Fiddlin' My Own Way : The Violet Hensley Story
Testing the Metal of Life : The Joe Barger Story
Stirring Up Success with a Southern Flavor

https://RandallFranks.com/Store

https://www.amazon.com/stores/Randall-Franks/author/B00K9XIDN4

SEEING FAITH
A DEVOTIONAL

RANDALL FRANKS

Learn more at
https://.RandallFranks.com/Seeing-Faith

About the Author

Actor/entertainer Randall Franks is best known as "Officer Randy Goode" from TV's "In the Heat of the Night," a role he performed on NBC and CBS from 1988–1993. A star of UPtv from 2009-2014, he appeared in several films and with Robert Townsend in the series "Musical Theater of Hope."

Randall Franks

© 2016 Randall Franks Media – Anna Ritch

He has co-starred or starred in 20 films with superstars including Dolly Parton, Christian Slater, William Hurt, Stella Parton, and legendary western star "Doc" Tommy Scott. His most recent film is "The Cricket's Dance" with Kristen Renton, Maurice Johnson, William Mark McCullough and Sandra Ellis Laferty. He shares in a Best Ensemble Cast Award for this film.

Franks' musical stylings have been heard in 150 countries and by more than 25 million Americans. He is the 2024-25 Josie Music Awards Musician of the Year – Fiddle. The Independent Country Music Hall of Fame member's musical career boasts 25 album releases, 53 singles, and over 200 recordings with artists from various genres. The International Bluegrass Music Museum Legend annually hosts the historic Grand Master Fiddler Championship for several years at the Country Music Hall of Fame and Museum in Nashville, Tenn. The award-winning fiddler's best-selling release, "Handshakes and Smiles," was a top-20 Christian music seller. Many of his albums were among the top-30 bluegrass recordings of their release year. The Atlanta Country Music Hall of Fame member shared a top country vocal collaboration with Grand Ole Opry stars the Whites. In addition to his solo performances, tours with his Hollywood Hillbilly Jamboree, and years of guest starring for the Grand Ole Opry, Franks is a former member of Bill Monroe's Blue Grass Boys and Jim and Jesse's Virginia Boys. He has performed with Jeff and Sheri Easter, the Lewis Family, the Marksmen Quartet, the Watkins Family, Elaine and Shorty, "Doc" Tommy Scott's Last Real Old Time Medicine Show, and Doodle and the Golden River Grass.

He is the former Vice Mayor and Council Chairman in Ringgold, Ga., and is Catoosa Citizens for Literacy chairman, which assists individuals in learning to read and pursuing a GED at its Catoosa County Learning Center near Ringgold. He is also president of the Share America Foundation, Inc. that provides the Pearl and Floyd Franks Scholarship to musicians continuing the traditional music of Appalachia. He is the Northwest Georgia Joint Economic Development Authority film industry liaison. He is the Georgia Production Partnership past vice president and serves on government relations committee.

He authored eleven other books, including "Seeing Faith: A Devotional," "Testing the Metal of Life: The Joe Barger Story" with Joe Barger, "A Badge or an Old Guitar: A Music City Murder Mystery;" "Encouragers I: Finding the Light;" "Encouragers II: Walking with the Masters;" "Encouragers III: A Guiding Hand;" "Whittlin' and Fiddlin' My Own Way: The Violet Hensley Story" with Violet Hensley; "A Mountain Pearl: Appalachian Reminiscing and Recipes;" "Stirring Up Success with a Southern Flavor," and "Stirring Up Additional Success with a Southern Flavor" with Shirley Smith; and "Snake Oil, Superstars and Me" with "Doc" Tommy Scott and Shirley Swiesz.

A journalist with more than 20 state and national awards, Franks is also a syndicated columnist with his "Southern Style" appearing weekly in newspapers from North Carolina to Texas and at randallfranks.com. He was included among his generation's leading country humorists in the Loyal Jones book "Country Music Humorists and Comedians."

For more information, visit www.randallfranks.com and www.shareamericafoundation.org.

Be sure to visit on the web:
Randall Franks on X
https://X.com/RandallFranks
Randall Franks Fan Page on Facebook
www.facebook.com/RandallFranksActorDirectorEntertainer
Randall Franks on YouTube:
http://www.youtube.com/@randallfranks
Randall Franks at IMDB:
http://www.imdb.com/name/nm0291684/

Randall Franks (left) as "Capt. Robert Shields" in "The American's Creed"
Learn more and Get the Film and Documentary at
https://RandallFranks.com/The-Americans-Creed

Watch Christian Films Featuring Randall Franks

Some Others:
Phoenix Falling
with Stella Parton
Firebase 9
The Cricket's Dance
The Flamingo Rising
with William Hurt
Blue Valley Songbird
with Dolly Parton

Watch Randall Franks TV
on
YouTube, Rumble
and Brighteon